TERROR A

"Give the lady bac[...] as his Colt .45 cleared leather.

Barnes and his men turned to stare at him, the beautiful Paulina Parker forgotten for the moment. Barnes spun Paulina's derringer in his hand and pointed it at Fargo. The rest of the men drew instantly.

Fargo did a quick count. Six bullets in his Colt. A dozen men aiming at him dead center. Yeah, the odds weren't great.

"Says who," Barnes spat. "We're just getting to know the lady."

"I don't like your manners," Fargo said, and pulled the trigger. His Colt rang out, a cloud of gunpowder rising around him. Barnes jumped back an instant after Fargo's bullet nipped his leather boot and left a hole in the floor.

"Next time I aim higher," the Trailsman said, with only five shots left, and twelve guns still on him, and the odds against him going from bad to damn fool. . . .

BE SURE TO READ THE OTHER
THRILLING NOVELS IN THE EXCITING
TRAILSMAN SERIES!

THE TRAILSMAN

#181

VENGEANCE AT DEAD MAN RAPIDS

by

Jon Sharpe

1943   9253

A SIGNET BOOK

SIGNET
Published by the Penguin Group
Penguin Books USA Inc., 375 Hudson Street,
New York, New York 10014, U.S.A.
Penguin Books Ltd, 27 Wrights Lane,
London W8 5TZ, England
Penguin Books Australia Ltd,
Ringwood, Victoria, Australia
Penguin Books Canada Ltd, 10 Alcorn Avenue,
Toronto, Ontario, Canada M4V 3B2
Penguin Books (N.Z.) Ltd, 182–190 Wairau Road,
Auckland 10, New Zealand

Penguin Books Ltd, Registered Offices:
Harmondsworth, Middlesex, England

First published by Signet, an imprint of Dutton Signet,
a division of Penguin Books USA Inc.

First Printing, January, 1997
10 9 8 7 6 5 4 3 2 1

The first chapter of this book originally appeared in *The Greenback
Trail*, the one hundred eightieth volume in this series.

Ⓟ REGISTERED TRADEMARK—MARCA REGISTRADA

Printed in the United States of America

The Trailsman

Beginnings . . . they bend the tree and they mark the man. Skye Fargo was born when he was eighteen. Terror was his midwife, vengeance his first cry. Killing spawned Skye Fargo, ruthless, cold-blooded murder. Out of the acrid smoke of gunpowder still hanging in the air, he rose, cried out a promise never forgotten.

The Trailsman they began to call him all across the West: searcher, scout, hunter, the man who could see where others only looked, his skills for hire but not his soul, the man who lived each day to the fullest, yet trailed each tomorrow. Skye Fargo, the Trailsman, and the seeker who could take the wildness of a land and the wanting of a woman and make them his own.

1860, in the land some call Arizona,
Where the mighty Colorado River rages
And bloodred rocks hide a secret village
Doomed by an ancient oath of revenge.

1

He spotted the town from a long distance away. It looked like a few wooden crates somebody had set down and forgotten on the middle of a wide red plain surrounded by buttes. As he came nearer, he counted seven rickety false-fronted buildings standing on either side of the trail. In the middle of Main Street, if you wanted to call it that since it was the only street, stood a water pump that hunched over the long wooden trough like a thirsty rusted vulture.

His lake-blue eyes smarted from the baking heat and the white glare of the long ride through the glittering alkali. Dust lay in the folds of his clothing, coated his face, his hands. His horse walked slowly between the small clutter of board structures, its thick hooves clopping on the packed dry earth, echoing in the silence of the town. When he got close to the water pump, he saw that next to it somebody had had the bright idea to put up a sign that read: NOWHERE, POPULATION 14.

He dismounted, pumped fresh water into the trough, and dashed some over his head and neck.

While his black and white pinto drank deeply from the trough, he glanced at the warped board buildings that clustered along the street with their dust-dim panes like empty eyes. The biggest building was two stories, gray siding flecked with peeling yellow paint, its shutters hanging askew. The sign read: WISKEE AN WEMEN. He scrutinized the dozen horses that stood tethered and glittering with sweat outside.

Nowhere. Yeah, that about summed it up all right. He'd arrived at the town of Nowhere for sure.

The pinto, muzzle dripping, raised its head and shook it as if agreeing with his unspoken assessment. He led the horse and tied it in the patch of shade to one side of the saloon, fed it the last carrot from his saddlebag. Whiskey and women. Yeah, he could use a long drink and some female company. The hinges of the bat-wing doors creaked in protest as he pushed inside.

The Nowhere Saloon was one big room with a few scattered chairs and tables about as rickety as the building itself. A long carved bar, nicked and scratched, was topped by a broken mirror and stood along one wall. The bartender, a lanky bald man with eyes like an old bloodhound, looked up as he entered and continued polishing a glass. The dozen men sitting at two large round tables at the rear laid down their cards and turned around in their chairs. They looked like a rough gang, trail-hardened and hungry as old wolves. One of them, a broad-shouldered big one with lanks of greasy black hair that hung down to his shoulders and a buckskin thong tied across his brow, pulled his pistol and waved it around.

He'd seen this kind before. One false move, one threatening gesture, and the pack of unruly ruffians would be on him in a second.

Skye Fargo had an iron-clad policy not to seek out trouble. In his experience, trouble found him eventually anyway. And tangling with this pack of bruisers would just delay him from the business at hand. He had a job to finish, and the wad of money in his jacket seemed to be burning a hole in the pocket. Yeah, he'd feel easier when the money was in the right hands and the job was done.

So Fargo took no notice of the dozen men staring as he walked across the wooden floor straight to the bar. But he saw them nonetheless, watching them from the corner of his eye for the least whisper of movement, his hand resting lightly on the butt of his Colt, the muscles of his lean body tensed and wary as a cougar's. He hooked his boot over the bar rail and felt their eyes still on him.

"What'll it be?" The bartender rubbed his bald pate nervously.

"Tequila. Salt."

The bartender pulled up a clear bottle with a white liquid and a long worm soaking in it, the real stuff out of Mexico, and poured a glass and set it down alongside a bowl of coarse salt. The men resumed their card game, and as Fargo swigged the liquor, they glanced warily over their shoulders from time to time.

11

"Never seen you before," the bartender said. He blinked his bloodhound eyes slowly, then took up another glass and began polishing it on his dirty apron.

"Never seen you, either," Fargo answered. The bartender shrugged, then grinned as he caught Fargo's wry smile and the gold coin he slid along the bar. "Name's Skye Fargo."

"The Trailsman," the bartender said, making no effort to hide his admiration. "Well, I'll be. Always wanted to catch a glimpse of you. My name's Sims. I heard tell all about you. I knowed you was somebody special when you walked in. Drinks on the house, mister."

"Keep it," Fargo said as Sims tried to return the coin. The men playing cards hadn't taken any notice of their conversation, and Fargo doubted they'd overheard the words. It was just as well. He preferred to travel incognito. "Maybe you can help me," Fargo added quietly as Sims poured him another tequila. "I'm looking for a man named Ed Dofield. A sheep man I think. You know where he'd be?"

"Sure, I know Ed Dofield. He'd be up on his ranch about a day's hard ride north. You follow the Little Colorado River north then cut across west before it gets to the Big Colorado and the canyon. His spread's east of the badlands and tucked up in those grass hills, just at the lip of the Big Canyon."

"Much obliged," Fargo said. He took a pinch of salt on his tongue, then polished off the tequila. It had been a long trail and a hard ride. Now it was almost over, and he was about to deliver the money Ed Dofield had been due for more than thirty years and collect his reward. Another job done. And then he was a free man until the next job. He never knew what the next job was going to be, but one thing was for certain—it always caught up to him in the form of trouble.

The card game was getting louder and more raucous. The bartender took the men a couple of bottles of whiskey, and they called out for a couple more. Two of them began arguing, shouting about an ace of diamonds, and Fargo thought it might come to blows, but then they settled down again. Fargo switched to ale and thought about his next move. The afternoon sunlight lengthened across the floor. He could stay in the town of Nowhere for the night, find a pretty woman, settle in a nice hot bath and a soft feather bed.

"The sign outside says, WOMEN," Fargo said.

"Used to be." Sims rubbed his bloodshot eyes and then rested his elbows on the bar. "Town's seen better days. Used to have three doves—purty ones, too, a stagecoach drop, and a sheriff. Now we ain't got none of 'em. Can't even get the mail on a regular basis."

"No sheriff?" Fargo asked. "Ain't that kind of dangerous?"

Sims pulled his hand out of one pocket and showed Fargo the butt of a pistol. "I keep the law and order in here. But out there"—nodded toward the door—"it's every man for himself."

No women. That made up his mind. There was

no point to staying in Nowhere for the night. Yeah, he'd ride on out, bathe in the Little Colorado River, and sleep under the wheeling stars. He'd just finished his last beer and had decided to leave when the jangle of bridles and the creak of leather reached his ears. Swift footsteps crossed the wooden porch outside, and the bat-wing doors creaked open.

Fargo turned to see a woman standing in the sunlight, blinking her eyes as she adjusted to the dimness inside the bar. Her hair was pulled back but the sun caught the wisps of blond curls around her face that lit up like a golden haze. She was small with a sturdy build, not heavy but round in the right places, and with piercing brown eyes. She was dressed in an Easterner's idea of Wild West clothes, a fringed buckskin skirt and jacket, fancy boots, and she carried a wide-brimmed hat in her hands.

The men at the card game reacted immediately. Several of them rose from their seats and whistled and clapped. She made her way to the bar, ignoring their catcalls. She hardly glanced at Fargo but addressed the bartender.

"Pardon me, sir," she said. "I'm Paulina Parker. Maybe you've heard of me, read my books. *A Hundred Nights on the Amazon*? Or maybe *Romance on the Nile?*" Sims gaped at her, too stunned to answer, so she went on. "Never mind. I'm trying to find somebody to sell me a boat. You know, for river travel. Like an Indian canoe. Anything like that here in this town?"

She had a hint of a Southern accent. Her voice was soft-edged like a little girl's, but Fargo also heard a note of firm determination in it. He glanced at her, taking in the curved lines of her form, the long golden braid of hair hanging down her back, the upturned tilt of her nose. She ignored his look.

Behind her, the dozen men were slowly walking toward the bar, listening to her every word. The big greasy one with the thong headband was licking his lips. Fargo spotted a man in the front in a stained leather hat who seemed to be their leader. He was a short wiry fellow with a shock of thick gray hair and eyes too close together. He was grinning ear to ear.

"Canoes," Sims said at last. "Canoes. Sure, lady. At the end of the street, ole Zeke's got a bunch he was trying to unload a few years ago. Got 'em stored out back in a sod hut. Bet he'd be glad to sell them to you."

"Wonderful. Thank you so much," Paulina said. She turned to go and stopped abruptly, surrounded by the men. Fargo's hand was on the butt of his Colt when she suddenly spoke. "Don't fuss with me, boys," she said. She fumbled at her waistband and suddenly a small derringer was glittering in her hand. The wiry man in front took a surprised step back and held up his hands with a laugh. They were all pretty drunk.

"Why, look here boys," he said, his speech slow and slightly slurred. "It's a lady spitfire." He doffed his hat with an exaggerated motion. "We were just coming over to introduce ourselves, welcome you to the territory."

"Well, thank you kindly," Paulina said. Fargo saw the derringer waver slightly. Yeah, she was putting up a good show, but she was scared all right. The bartender was standing back from the bar, watching warily.

"I'm Barnes, Cavell Barnes," the wiry man said, replacing the hat on his head. "And these are my friends."

"I'm Platan Arnez, m'am," the big headband piped up. He was silenced by a look from Barnes.

"Why don't you just come have a little refreshment with us, pretty lady?" Barnes said smoothly. There was a long silence as the derringer hovered in the air, pointed at Barnes' chest. Fargo calculated the odds. A dozen men, some he could take out, some he couldn't because Paulina was in his line of fire.

"No thanks, Mister Barnes," she said. "I'm kind of in a hurry. Another time."

She started to back away toward the door but Cavell Barnes took a step to follow her, then reached out to the derringer. Paulina drew back and seemed to hesitate about pulling the trigger. Barnes was too quick for her, and in a moment he'd wrested it from her and held it on his open palm.

"Now, ain't this a pretty thing?" he said, speaking to the derringer, then looking Paulina over head to toe. This had gone far enough. Fargo's Colt was in his hand.

"Give the lady her gun back." At the sound of

his voice, Barnes and his men turned to stare at him. Barnes spun the derringer in his hand and pointed it at Fargo. The rest of the men drew instantly. Six bullets in his Colt. A dozen men all aiming at him dead center. Yeah, the odds weren't great. It could turn into a bloodbath any moment.

"Says who?" Barnes spat. "We're just getting to know the lady." Behind him, Fargo heard Sims pull up a pistol to back him up. So now there were twelve bullets against twelve men. Barnes squinted at them. Paulina's chest was heaving as her breaths came quickly. "I don't like your manners," Fargo said. For a moment he considered Cavell Barnes' shin, imagined a bullet in it. Yeah, it was tempting to wing him. Or maybe his big toe. But that might start 'em shooting. He decided a warning shot would drive them off.

Fargo pulled the trigger, and his Colt rang out, a cloud of gunpowder rising around him. Cavell jumped back an instant after Fargo's bullet nipped a chunk of his leather boot and left a hole in the floor. Fargo vaulted sideways and grabbed Paulina around the waist, pulling her back with him and pushing her down beneath him behind the bar. Where he'd stood an instant before, three bullets split the wood of the bar. Sims had ducked for cover.

"Next time I aim higher," Fargo said, covering them with his Colt. Sims took courage and reappeared alongside him from behind the bar like a prairie dog coming up from his hole. "Now, let's have the lady's gun. And get the hell out." Barnes hesitated and then realized he and his men were yards from any table they might use for cover. Meanwhile Fargo and Sims could pick them off from behind the bar. The odds weren't in his favor now.

"Sure," Barnes said, tossing it toward him. It landed on the floor and discharged, the bullet flying wide.

"Shit!" one of the men yelled, grabbing his arm. The bullet had grazed his flesh. Barnes ignored the disruption.

"Sure. We're going. But we ain't going to forget this, Mister Skye Fargo." Fargo exchanged surprised glances with the bartender. Barnes headed toward the door with the rest of his men following and spoke over his shoulder. "Yeah, I know who you are. Recognized you when you walked in, Trailsman. We'll be looking for you. I never forget an unkindness to me and my boys."

The men piled out the door, and in a moment the room was deserted. Fargo helped Paulina to her feet and retrieved her derringer.

"Thank you so much, Mister . . . Mister Fargo was it?" she said, her manners a little formal but her words sincere. She stuck out her hand and Fargo took it, small in his and cool to the touch. He let it go reluctantly, realizing he was damn hungry for female company. "I'm Paulina Parker. Author. Maybe you've read my books—*A Hundred Nights on the Amazon*? And—"

"*Romance on the Nile*," he finished for her.

"You *have* read my books!? You've actually read them?"

"No, I just heard you mention them to Sims here," Fargo said. The bartender offered her a drink, and she took a glass of beer. They settled down at a table. "What in hell brings you out here?"

"My next book," she said enthusiastically. "*Down the Raging Colorado*. I'm going to be the first person ever to canoe down the Big Canyon—some folks call it the Grand Canyon. I hear it's one of the wonders of the world. I can't wait to see it and write all about it. It will be my best book ever. Now that I'm this far, all I need is a canoe and some supplies."

"And more lives than a cat," Fargo said. "The white water in that canyon will chew you up and spit you out in a hundred tiny pieces. You aim your boat six inches too far in one direction and you're done for, smashed to smithereens on a rock sharp as a bear tooth. There's a reason why nobody's ever tried going down that river before. It's just plain crazy. You want to get somewhere in this territory, you get on a horse and ride there."

"Sounds like you know an awful lot about it," she said, seemingly undaunted by his words. She sipped her beer, pulled the braid over her shoulder, and smiled at him. Damned pretty. "Maybe you could tell me what kind of canoe I need. I was thinking birch bark might be lightest and easier to carry for portage. You know, sometimes you have to carry the canoe around the rapids that are too rough."

"You do know something about it," Fargo said. So she wasn't completely ignorant. But the whole idea seemed lunatic. "Just take my advice and don't try birch bark. That river will snap it like a toothpick at the first rapid. You want a solid wood boat, low and wide with a flat keel to get over the shallows."

He stopped to watch as she took a tiny leather notebook from her skirt pocket, pulled out a small nib pen and ink bottle, dipped the pen, and wrote something into the book.

"What else?" she asked, looking up at him with a blinding smile.

"Get somebody to hammer a sheet of tin"—he pointed up at the embossed tin ceiling—"like that, over the bottom. And get a cover, some canvas, over the top, so when the water pours in you don't swamp and sink." He paused as she continued to scribble into her notebook. "And get some air pockets built in fore and aft, animal stomachs will do, to keep her afloat, too. But there's one piece of advice I can give you that is the most important thing, the thing you really ought to listen to—"

"Do tell," Paulina said, taking in his every word.

"Forget the whole goddamn thing," Fargo said. "Forget trying to canoe down the Colorado River. You're going to die trying. And that would be a waste of one beautiful woman."

She snapped the notebook shut, blushed at his compliment, and turned away for a moment. Damn, she was pretty and an unusual woman with an indomitable spirit. Either that or she was just plumb loco. Maybe a little of both.

"You see, I just *have* to go," she said, putting away the pen and ink. "I've been like this all my life. I want to experience everything, try everything, have adventures. I've climbed the pyramids in Egypt. I went on a raft down the Amazon River and saw those wild people who are cannibals and shrink human heads." She shuddered. "We almost didn't get away that time. Another time, we tried to cross Canada from Nova Scotia to Alaska, but we got caught by the early snows and had to hole up for the rest of the winter."

"Who's this *we*?" Fargo said. Yeah, he'd thought she was unattached. He'd got his hopes up there for a moment.

"Oh, that's Bishy," Paulina said. "Aloisha Bishy, my traveling companion. He's come on all my trips. He's so helpful." A sudden cloud came over her expression. "He ought to be along. Said he'd just water the horses."

A sound of shouting drew their attention, and Fargo rose and ran out of the saloon, followed closely by Paulina. The street was filled with Barnes' men on their horses, and it was clear the fight had just broken out. The tall headband named Platan Arnez had lassoed somebody, looked like an old man, and was dragging him the length of the street while Barnes and the others hooted and hollered from their horses. The old man was already bloody and battered, and it looked like they were fixing to drag him right out of town behind them.

"Bishy!" Paulina screamed.

Fargo drew his Colt and fired in an instant, the bullet slicing through the rope. The form of the old man suddenly lay still in the dusty street as Barnes and his horsed men rode on. Fargo fired again, and Platan Arnez plummeted forward onto the neck of his horse, clutching his arm. Several of Barnes' men turned and fired back. Barnes shouted something unintelligible but furious, and in another moment they'd ridden out of town.

"Bastards!" Paulina screamed after them. Her derringer was in her hand, but she hadn't fired. She ran toward the figure in the street, and Fargo followed, keeping his ears alert in case Barnes and his gang might decide to double back and make more trouble.

Paulina knelt down on the ground and cradled Bishy's head in her lap. Fargo loosened the lasso and freed his hands. After a moment the old man came around, rubbed his eyes, and groaned.

"Oh, hell, Paulina," he said as his eyelids fluttered and he saw her face over him. "You get us in the worst messes."

"What happened?" Her voice was tender and angry at the same moment.

"That pack of dogs came out of the saloon and asked me if I knew you, and I said I been traveling with you for five years now. Before I knew what was happening, they started sweeping the damn street with my belly.

Fargo gave Bishy a hand to his feet, and they walked him over to the water pump, where he cleaned up, washing the blood and dust off. He wasn't hurt too bad, some nasty abrasions on his hands and a scratch on his cheek, his clothing torn up. Grizzled hair flew about his head like a white cloud, and his long beard hung halfway down his chest. His blue eyes were pale, as if faded by the sun, and his skin was weather-rough.

Fargo introduced himself and, at the sound of his name, Bishy sat down on the side of the trough in amazement.

"Well, if that don't beat everything," Bishy said, scratching his head. "I can't believe it. Once again, Paulina Parker's amazing luck." He spoke to her, but nodded his head toward Fargo. "You know, you just happened to run into the best damn trail-finder in the West. Knows the ways of the wild as good as a redskin. Hires himself out to folks that need help. I was just telling you we needed to get us some help to navigate that Grand Canyon water. And here you go running into the only man in the West that can get us through there alive!" Bishy chuckled. "Damn if that don't beat everything, Paulina. I never seen such luck in one person."

"Wonderful!" Paulina clapped her hands. "A trail-finder! I had no idea you were for hire, Mister Fargo! Oh, this is wonderful, this is perfect!" She clapped her hands again.

"Sorry," Fargo said. "I'm not your man. I'm not a tour guide." Paulina subsided into disappointment at his words and started to interrupt but he continued. "I don't hire out for adventurers. I don't go taking on trouble for the purpose of helping people risk their lives. I don't do anything just for the hell of it. And I'm not for sale."

"But I could pay you well," Paulina said. "I'll pay you very well. Say, two thousand dollars? My last book made lots of money and—"

"No," Fargo said. "No. And that's final. I don't just work for money. I have to believe what I'm doing is important. Something that needs doing. Good luck getting down the Grand Canyon, but I won't be a party to going off on some kind of whim, getting yourself killed for nothing."

"My books aren't nothing!" Paulina snapped. She wheeled about and stalked off toward two horses tethered beside the saloon and began pulling some things out of her saddlebag.

"She's got a lot of spunk, ain't she?" Bishy said as the two of them watched her march toward a small battered building with a faded sign that read: THE GRAND HOTEL.

"Sure has," Fargo said.

"And she's the luckiest person I ever knew." Bishy said, shaking his head. "Why, if I told you half the things I been through with her, you'd call me a damn liar to my face. Rampaging cannibals chasing us through a jungle. A Turkish sultan kidnapping her for his harem. A hundred spear-carrying Watusis on the warpath in Africa. She's just got that knack of getting out of a tight spot. Every time she gets in trouble some damn thing always happens, and she gets out by the skin of her teeth. And then on she goes getting herself into more trouble. I never seen anything like it in my life."

Fargo grinned to himself. Interesting woman, he decided. Spirit, fire, beauty, intelligence. Good combination. Too bad she'd got her mind set on committing suicide trying to run the rapids of the Colorado River.

She reappeared at the doorway of what was called the hotel, and called out, "Come on, Bishy! We're going down here to a man named Zeke to get us a canoe. I got us rooms for tonight. We'll set out tomorrow."

Fargo watched her walk down the street, followed by Bishy. She didn't look back. He patted the wad of money in his pocket, thinking of the day's ride north to Ed Dofield's Circle D Ranch, the job he had to finish, thinking of the cold-water bath he'd promised himself in the Little Colorado River, of the chill clear night air as he would sleep under the stars. Get a move on, he told himself. But instead, he found himself walking into the hotel.

He carried out a conversation with himself the whole time he signed the hotel register, ordered a hot bath sent up, took the keys to his room, and went to stable the Ovaro. Maybe just maybe, he told himself as he brushed the trail dust from the pinto's gleaming coat, he could talk Paulina Parker out of this crazy plan of hers. Or find some other way to persuade her not to get herself killed. Some method of persuasion they'd both enjoy. There was more than one way to save a life.

*   *   *

Paulina seemed genuinely glad to see him when he appeared that evening in the saloon and had clearly forgotten her last angry words. She was still dressed in the buckskins but now had on a red shirt and had loosed her golden hair which fell over her shoulders in sinuous glittering waves. He'd taken a nice long soak in a hot tub and changed into fresh jeans and a denim shirt. Much as he hated towns, civilization did have a few advantages. But in the town of Nowhere, the food wasn't one of them.

For the next hour, he dined with Paulina and Bishy on steaks tough as saddle leather, soggy potatoes, and rot-gut coffee. The apple pie was sour. Sims apologized for the food, explaining they didn't get supplies very often.

Throughout the evening Fargo had been on edge, listening for any sound of men on horseback, wondering when and if Cavell Barnes and his men would ride back into town. Barnes said he'd be looking for Fargo, said he'd not forget. And over the years he'd seen a lot of men like Cavell Barnes. They didn't forget.

By the time they'd finished the meal, Bishy excused himself. He was bruised and sore from his encounter with the Barnes gang and eager to sink into a feather bed and give his old bones some rest. He limped off. Fargo ordered two brandies. Sims dug around behind the bar and came up with a dust-covered bottle. He poured two glasses of the honey-colored liquor. Fargo raised his glass to Paulina, then took a sip: He knew fine brandy when he tasted it, and he smiled with pleasure.

"Yeah, this makes up for the meal. It's the real thing," he said. "French. From around the Cognac region. Aged in oak maybe seven years or so. You can taste oak, but it's subtle. It's just right. Perfectly balanced." He swirled it in the glass, took another sip, and sucked some air into his mouth to enjoy the complex fumes.

Paulina summoned Sims and asked to look at the bottle. She looked up from reading the label, her brown eyes full of appreciation.

"Exactly right," she said. "I like a man who knows what he's talking about. No bullshit—if you'll excuse my language." There was a silence as she regarded him across the table. He reached across and took her hand, raised it to his lips, and kissed the palm, then the inside of her tender wrist. Her skin smelled sweet, some kind of spring flower he couldn't place. Violets maybe? Startled, she withdrew her hand.

He ignored it and took another sip of cognac, then asked her about her adventures. Two hours later they were still talking. She'd been a lot of places for sure, seen a lot of the world, and braved a lot of dangers, all because she wanted to be a world-famous author. She saw the trip down the Grand Canyon as her big break. That's why she wanted to go so badly.

"But what about you?" she asked. "I'm sorry I didn't recognize your name, but Bishy tells me you're really famous. He says everybody in the West knows you. Why don't you write a book about your adventures?"

"I'm too busy having 'em," Fargo said. "I like to live my life, and I don't need to tell other people about it." Paulina subsided into silence, and Fargo thought he might have offended her. "But, everybody's got a different reason to do what they're doing," he added.

"Why *do* you do what you're doing?" Paulina asked. "This trailblazing, this wandering? Why do you do it?"

Fargo had asked himself that question many a time. It was impossible to explain to her in words the way the land pulled at him, the way the open trail lured him, the joy he felt with the trusty Ovaro galloping beneath him. It was impossible to tell her how the mountain peaks spoke, called to him. How a lone eagle floating in the blue sky seemed to be a sign to ride on through the miles of dark forests, waving grasslands, searing desert. Something told him that someday civilization would spread throughout the West, that the little settlements would become towns and then cities, would fill the wild lands and roads would crisscross it like so many ropes. Some people said the West would never be tamed, but Fargo knew in his heart that they were kidding themselves.

And then there were the troubles that found him—the father whose daughter was taken off by *bandidos*. The town overrun by a gang of no-goods. A woman in search of a treasure so she could save a mission orphanage. A tribe of Indians being cheated out of their hunting grounds. A family held hostage. Yeah, trouble always found him. He came out of his reverie to realize she was studying his face as if she could read his every thought.

"I understand," she said, and Fargo knew she did. They had something in common. She had her adventures for her reason and he for his. But in some way they were alike. He reached for her hand, and she gave it reluctantly. He stroked it with his fingers, lightly, promising more. Her brown eyes were wide, and he read something there.

"You're scared, aren't you?" he said. Paulina swallowed and blushed.

"No."

"Yes," he said. "Yes, you are scared. You said you like experience. You're always looking for adventure." She tried to remove her hand from his grasp, but he held onto it.

"It doesn't include that kind of . . . of adventure."

"Why not? It's part of enjoying life." He let go of her hand. She put both hands in her lap, out of his reach. "It's like this brandy here," Fargo said, taking another sip and rolling it over his tongue. "The more you know about it, the more experience you have of it, the more you appreciate the really good stuff."

He saw her eyes widen as she took this in, and he wondered if she were a virgin. Maybe, despite all her adventures, she'd never even enjoyed the pleasures of the body. It was possible.

"I think it's time to go," Paulina announced, standing up suddenly.

Fargo paid Sims for the dinner and drinks, and followed her out the door. The town of Nowhere

29

was dark and still. Countless stars glittered overhead in the cold and clear desert night, seeming close enough to touch.

"How beautiful," Paulina breathed as she stood in the dark street looking up at them. A coyote barked nearby, and she jumped, huddling close to him. He laughed and put one arm around her, felt her stiffen a little at his touch, and then slowly relaxed as he made no further move.

To the east, he saw a pale glow in the sky. Almost moonrise, always a spectacular moment in the desert night. "Got something to show you," he said, walking her to the eastern edge of town.

They stood waiting in the cold night breeze, looking expectantly toward the horizon. The desert night was full of small noises, the yip of the coyotes, distant song of a lone wolf and flap of a bat overhead. They heard a two-note coo, the night call of the burrowing owl. He identified all the sounds for her. Then, between two buttes, the edge of the moon appeared, a white dome that grew swiftly larger, flooding the desert with a light that seemed almost blinding, a huge milk-white moon, mysterious and pocked. It rose above the horizon, and she shivered. He drew her close, and she glanced up at him.

Then his mouth was on hers and her lips, shy, hesitant, opened to take his tongue in, her sweetness like honey. He caressed her back as she clung to him, opening to him, hungry, and he felt her loneliness, her want. His hands tangled in the surges of her silken hair, and he kissed her again,

again, bent to kiss her neck, inhaling the violet sweetness of her, enjoying the warm softness of her curved hips and back beneath his hands. Suddenly she withdrew, pulled away from him.

"I think I'd best be getting back," she said stiffly. She wouldn't look at him or take his arm. They returned to the hotel in silence. He followed her up the creaking staircase and down the hallway. A flickering oil lamp stood on a small table next to the door of her room. The key was trembling in her hand so much that she couldn't put it into the lock. He took it from her, inserted it into the keyhole, pushed open the door, and then stepped back. She'd have to invite him in. But she stepped through the door and didn't look back.

"Good night, Skye." He heard the note of regret in her voice and without meeting his gaze, she shut the door behind her. And locked it. For a moment he stood listening to the creak of her footsteps inside the room as she got ready for bed.

He thought up a string of silent curses. There was no understanding women. He blew out the oil lamp. Moonlight poured through the window at the end of the hallway as he made his way to his room. He hadn't forgotten Barnes and his gang. All night he'd been on edge, listening and watching, even as he'd enjoyed Paulina's companionship. And before he opened the door to his room, he stood listening, just in case some of those bastards had sneaked back into town and were waiting to jump him. He opened the door wide, but there was no one inside.

The silvery moonlight lay across the white coverlet of the brass bed. He stripped down to the skin, stowed his Colt beneath his pillow, and eased his long muscular body between the sheets, enjoying the coolness of the fresh cotton, the pillowy soft cloud of the thick feather bed beneath him.

He had almost drifted into sleep when he heard the floorboards creak, a door open. He was alert in a moment, his hand under the pillow reaching for the Colt. Then he smiled, and he placed the pistol on his bedside table. There was a light tap at his door. He smiled to himself and laid the pistol on the bedside table. He pulled the bedsheet around him and opened the door to find her standing there dressed in a white nightgown with ruffles at the high neck and long sleeves. Her golden hair cascaded down her shoulders, her eyes were lowered, and he saw she was trembling.

"I am scared," she said.

He pulled her gently inside and shut the door behind her.

"This adventure won't be dangerous," he said. "And you'll enjoy it. I promise."

2

"You were right, Skye," Paulina said again. "I'm scared." She still wouldn't look up at him. The moonlight caught in her hair and glinted here and there like pale stars. She seemed to float all white in her cotton gown against the bare white of the walls.

He pulled her close to him and bent to kiss her, nibbling gently at her soft lips, savoring the fresh sweetness of her lips and the scent that rose from her warm flesh, from inside the white gown, like a crowd of spring violets in the fresh morning air.

She was scared, hesitant, her hands tentatively stroking his back at first. His tongue explored her mouth, his hands gently cradled her head and slowly explored her back, the softness of her hips. Slowly. He'd take it slowly but he felt himself hard as a rock, thinking of possessing her, and she felt it, too, shifted away shyly. She was so different from the buckskin-clad woman who had boldly pointed the derringer at Cavell Barnes that afternoon.

"Where's that fearless explorer?" he whispered in her ear.

Paulina giggled, and he led her toward the bed

with the sheet still wound around him. She turned her back as he started to take it off. He grinned and slid under the patchwork quilt. She sat on the other side of the bed, her back still to him. He lay looking up at the shadows on the pressed tin ceiling and waited. Women came when they wanted to, there was no hurrying them. And it was sweeter that way.

After a moment she pulled the gown off over her head and crept under the quilt, snuggling against his side. And then they were kissing again, fused suddenly as one, his tongue deep inside her, his hands exploring her, covering her soft full breasts, the nipples knotting with desire. She moaned and shivered as he stroked slowly down her rib cage, then brushed his hands across her belly, lightly on the soft furry mons, then across her thighs.

"Oh, yes, Skye. Yes, yes." Paulina was breathing heavily, and he guided her hand down to touch him. She grasped him, caught her breath, then stroked the length of him, slowly. "Oh, God. Yes."

He threw back the covers and gazed at her lying beneath him in the moonlight, her pale softness a feast of breasts as round as ripe fruit, nipples like strawberries, the delicate curve of her hips, and the pale fur between her legs. He flicked his tongue teasingly across one nipple, then took it into his mouth. She cried out in surprise and grasped the bars of the brass bed, writhing. He kissed downward, across the whiteness of her belly, then parted her thighs with his hands. The folds of her glistened, and her eyes widened in surprise. She gasped as he took her in his mouth, sucking and savoring her like a glass of fine liquor, his tongue now fast now slow, his hands grasping her soft breasts, kneading them gently.

Paulina could not control herself, and tried to muffle her cries in a pillow. She writhed back and forth, and he felt her harden, like the tiny pit of a juicy peach, and then she shuddered, trembling uncontrollably, her hips thrusting under his mouth. He rose above her, and her thighs fell open to him, the darkness welcoming him in, fragrant, palpitating, hot and ready. He pushed slowly, feeling her widen.

She gasped once, then smiled up at him as he began to stroke inside her, his huge rod filling her satiny sheath, deeper and deeper as she lifted her legs to open to him more fully. He kissed her deeply, fused again with her, lost in the torrents of pleasure, not knowing whose tongue was whose, whose hips were thrusting, who moaned. Paulina under him, around him, through him, her violet perfume filled his head, he swelled to fill all of her inside, felt the gathering, the inevitable coming begin to drive him. He slowed, slowed, made himself slow down, propped himself on his elbows and pumped into her, feeling the knot of her again, concentrating on her. She was close again, yes, he could feel the tension rising in her, her breath ragged. She grasped him around the neck and pulled him down as she tensed with a profound quake that shook her, and he felt her contract in spasms around him, squeezing him, and he came, spraying into her great gusts of himself, giving it to her again, again, deeper and deeper in a fury of ecstasy, a flurry of breasts and lips and tangled hair and eyes and hips, pounding and pumping, until he was spent. And then he slowed, stopped moving, lay on top of her for a long moment, holding her beneath him as if to keep her safe forever.

He rolled off onto his side. Paulina nestled under his arm, and the moonlight played in the tangled brightness of her long hair that spread out around them.

"Thank you, Skye," she murmured.

"You wanted experience and adventure," he teased her, tickling her chin. "Now are you going to write that up in your book?"

"Ummmm." Her eyelids were heavy. "I mean, no," she murmured. "Ummmm, I had no idea, no idea it would be so wonderful." She drifted off into sleep. Fargo put the Colt under his pillow again and lay listening to her soft breathing, the silence of the night. A horse whinnied from the direction of the stable. He listened for any other sounds, but there were none. He couldn't sleep. He got up and checked the lock on the door, stood by the window looking out at the deserted town and the moon, now high in the black night sky.

Somehow he had to convince her not to try this foolhardy thing. He'd seen the white water of the Colorado River from high above. He'd stood on the rim of the Grand Canyon, that inconceivably vast gash in the land, and he'd looked a mile down into the earth to see the white foaming of the river, the mighty river that had chewed away at the dust and the rock, eating its way downward. Years ago, he'd seen some foolhardy men try to take a line of five canoes down Marble Canyon, the white-walled gash upstream of the Big One. He'd followed along on his horse and watched as, one after another, their flimsy canoes hit rock after rock and broke apart. The last one sank just ten miles downstream of where they'd started, and no one had survived. The bastards hadn't known a thing about white water, hadn't followed Fargo's advice to take some heavier boats, didn't know how to shoot for the glassy V of water in the chutes between the rocks. No, they didn't know jack shit about white-water travel, and every damn one of them drowned.

He glanced back at the bed. And Paulina was going to try that same foolhardiness. Risk her life just to write a book. It seemed pretty silly to him. He'd try to talk some sense into her at breakfast.

"So you won't help me," Paulina said, pouting.

He mopped up the last of the syrup on his plate with a bite of pancake and chased it with a swig of coffee. Breakfast at the Nowhere Saloon was a damned sight better than the supper because he'd pulled some supplies, including fresh coffee, out of his saddlebag and rustled it up himself, with Paulina's and Bishy's help. They'd invited Sims to eat with them, and now he sat rubbing his bald head, his hound dog eyes thoughtful.

"Every man I heered tell tried to go down that river," Sims said, "well, every danged one of 'em hung up his hide or put a mighty big window in his skull one way or another. Even if you do get lucky and survive the river, there's lots else down there in that hellhole that'll kill you."

"Sounds like it will make a great book!" Paulina said. "Come on Skye. *You* ain't scared now, are you?" She gave him a wink.

"I'd go if there was a good reason for it," Fargo said. "But writing a book for a bunch of Easterners sitting in their comfy armchairs ain't a good reason as far as I can see."

"I think Mr. Fargo's made it pretty clear he's not coming," Bishy said, pouring more syrup on his stack. "You sure you don't want to reconsider? Listen, Paulina, we've been a lot of dangerous places. But maybe this Grand Canyon is too much to handle. How about let's climb Pike's Peak?"

"But that's been *done* already," Paulina complained. "No, it's settled. And I got everything underway. This man Zeke is hammering some tin on the bottom of a good thick boat and fitting it up just like you told me, Skye. I'm sure it'll be fine."

Try as he might, Fargo realized, nothing would dissuade her from this journey. At least not this morning. And he had to get moving himself, deliver this money to Ed Dofield at the Circle D Ranch.

"What's your hurry, Paulina?" Fargo said. "Let me reconsider the offer. I've got some business to finish, but I'll be back here in two or three days. You rest up, get your canoe ready. We'll talk about it when I get back."

"Okay, Skye," she said. There was something in her voice that was suddenly cool and distant. Did she believe him? She took a sip of her coffee, her dark eyes steady on him.

Well, he'd done his best, he told himself. And when he got back to the town of Nowhere, he'd try to think of another way to convince her. He rose and said his good-byes, then leaned over to kiss Paulina deeply. She responded warmly. Bishy sputtered his coffee, surprised, his pale blue eyes shocked and then laughing. Fargo left the saloon.

In the late afternoon, the sun was a blazing bronze sphere hung in the cloudless sky, as Fargo and the Ovaro began to climb the long gradual slope of land. All that day he'd kept watch for Cavell Barnes and his men, avoiding places where it would be easy to get ambushed. But he saw no one. He'd crossed searing alkali flats and dry beds of tortuous rivers thick with scorching sand. The empty burned plains had seemed never ending, hour after hour, and the distant flat–topped hills sliced with colored stripes and carved into fantastical shapes seemed to remain motionless as the pinto galloped mile after mile, until he'd come to the Little Colorado River and forded it. And then the land began to rise, slowly as he headed northeast toward the Circle D Ranch. Patches of tufted yellow grass appeared, pocked by dark hillocks of black volcanic scree. The sunlight shone through the white burst blossoms of the chollas with their dark stems, and in the distance he spotted a line of darkness, low piñon pines on the horizon where the land rose up above the badlands. He galloped on, toward the lip of the Grand Canyon.

By the time the sun touched down in the west, he'd found the Circle D ranch. It was a nice compound of substantial log buildings on the edge of a grassy clearing. A few sheep were penned in one corral and a fine bunch of horses in another. The meadow was surrounded by scraggly piñon pines and cedar with their shredded red bark strips fluttering like flags in the steady breeze. It was a good spot, plenty of grazing all around, at least for sheep. A man came out of the main house and then spotted him, and shouted a welcoming hello.

As Fargo rode toward him, he noticed the rancher wasn't even wearing a gun. He was a short stocky fellow with a friendly face and iron–gray hair.

"You Ed Dofield?" Fargo asked.

"Sure am."

Fargo swung down from the Ovaro and pulled the leather packet of money from his pocket.

"Got something for you." He handed it over.

Ed Dofield looked puzzled, then opened the leather packet, and his face was shocked. He began counting the bills, then looked up in astonishment.

"It's from your brother," Fargo said. Ed Dofield's face darkened. "I ran into him up in Canada, and he got shot. As he was dying, he told me he'd cheated you, owed you some money from way back. Said he'd lost touch with you, and he regretted it. Left you this note."

He handed a crumpled piece of paper to Ed Dofield. It wasn't a long note because the dying man hadn't had much strength. But Dofield swallowed hard when he read it, then glanced up searchingly into Fargo's face.

"Your brother hired me to get this money out of a bank in Sacramento," Fargo continued. "And then to find you and deliver it. So here it is. There's fifteen thousand dollars in there. I counted it out myself." Ed Dofield scratched his head in astonishment.

"Note says I owe you a thousand dollars for bringing me this money." Dofield counted out the bills, but Fargo saw he didn't stop at a thousand, but went on to two. He handed the stack of money over. "Occurs to me a lot of men would have disappeared with all that money. I always pay an honest man a bonus."

"Thank you," Fargo said, folding the money into his pocket.

"You telling me you rode all the way from Canada down to Sacramento and then found me out here in the middle of nothing?"

Ed Dofield laughed and something about his cackle made Fargo laugh, too. He introduced himself. "Skye Fargo himself? Well, that about beats all," Dofield said. "Harriet! Harriet!" A kind-looking woman appeared in the doorway. "Put on our best mutton tonight. We're going to have a helluva party."

Ed Dofield was as good as his word. In the close comfort of the sturdy ranch house, Dofield and his wife Harriet served up a meal of roast lamb with mint jelly and garlic, fresh green peas, and summer squash, a bottle of Kentucky bourbon they'd been saving for a special occasion, and a half dozen pies. Dofield's ranch hands joined in.

That night, Fargo fell asleep in the bunkhouse under a thick wool blanket thinking of Paulina and looking forward to being back in Nowhere with her. She'd be bound to see reason, he thought.

After breakfast, Ed Dofield insisted on taking Fargo on a tour of his ranch before he rode out. First they took a look inside the big barn and the storehouses. Everything was in perfect order from the stacks of hay bales to sheep-shearing implements and crates of supplies. In one storehouse there was even an old wooden boat that Dofield claimed he'd found once down on the riverbank.

As they got on their horses to ride around the ranch, Dofield admired the Ovaro and even made Fargo an offer for it, but said he understood completely when Fargo wouldn't even consider selling. It was a fine morning, the coolness of the dawn already edging toward heat, and they cantered together through the piñons and scrub oak, finding the grassy meadows thick with herds of grazing sheep.

"Sure is a strange thing to be a rich man all of a sudden," Ed Dofield wondered aloud.

"Probably be a good idea to put that money in a bank or else buy some more land with it," Fargo advised.

"I'll do that," Dofield agreed. "But first I'm just going to leave it setting spread out on the table for a few days so we can enjoy the sight of it. Never seen so much money in all my life. Never needed money before really, because we got rich land here. Can't grow nothing on it to speak of. And it's no good for cattle, neither. But it's rich for sheep anyways. Only problem is, it gets awfully lonely up here. You're the first visitor we've had in two year's time."

That reminded Fargo of Cavell Barnes and his men. He told of his encounter with the gang, and Ed Dofield said he'd pass the word to his ranch hands to keep an eye out in case they passed that way. At the edge of a scruffy gray sage plain that descended toward the badlands, they parted. By evening, he'd be back in Nowhere with the aggravating and beautiful Paulina Parker in his arms.

The sun was high overhead now and poured down in blistering streams. After a few hours he reached the beginning of a weird formation of red rocks that rose up like twisted towers from the flat alkali plain. The rock towers went on and on in a meandering line across the cracked plain, like the spiny back of a gigantic dragon buried in the desert sand. He dismounted and led the Ovaro to a patch of shade. He pulled the canteen from his saddle, took a swig, then poured some into his hat for the pinto. He had just put the water-cooled hat back on his head and was preparing to mount, when a sound reached his ears. Human.

Another man would have missed it, wouldn't have caught the faint moan among the distant rocks. But Fargo's acute sense of hearing picked it up immediately. Silently, he dropped the reins of the pinto. The Colt was in his hand as he moved forward, every muscle tense with readiness, his ears alert, his eyes scanning the twisted rocks that loomed above him like strange faces. His boots made the barest whisper. He paused beside a rock and waited, hearing the faint hiss of the wind blowing the thin layer of sand that lay on the hard-packed earth beneath his feet. A movement above caught his eye, and he glanced up to see a hawk wheeling high overhead. Its sharp eyes had spotted something below that looked promising, something dead or dying. The vultures would follow. It was bound to be close by. Then he heard the moan again, very close.

He rounded a rock tower silently, his gun at the ready. An open space between the rock towers opened to his view. In the center lay a man, an Indian. He was tall, well built, and muscular, wearing just a leather breechcloth and was tied with thick leather thongs spread-eagle to four wooden stakes driven deep into the hard soil. The Indian was gagged and around his neck was tied a rawhide band. He spotted Fargo, and his dark eyes flared with hope and with a plea.

Fargo stood considering for a moment. Whoever had done this might have good reason to. He'd seen that kind of rawhide band used before. It was a means of torture used by some of the Indian tribes hereabouts. You wet it and tied it tight around your enemy's throat, then left him out in the sun for a day. Two at most. The heat dried the leather, which slowly, very slowly shrank, cutting off the breath. Your enemy had lots of time to panic, lots of time to suffer and gasp. It was the kind of death that took hours and hours of slow agony.

It was impossible to tell whether the Indian who lay there deserved what he was getting. From the looks of him, Fargo guessed he was Havasupai, belonging to the tribe that lived far to the west at the bottom of the Grand Canyon. The Havasupai was a little-known tribe that didn't often leave their home. Their tribal name meant "people of the blue water," and they were generally peaceful. He'd met the Havasupai once long ago at the edge of the canyon and had found out about the tribe, learned a few words of their language. Now he wondered what this man's story could be.

Fargo walked once around the staked Havasupai as the Indian followed him with his eyes. Then he began trying to speak through the gag. After a moment Fargo decided to at least loosen the gag and hear what the man had to say. He'd just knelt down and was untying it when the Indian began to make loud noises, his eyes wide with terror and his head lolling back and forth.

It was probably due to the noise the Indian was making that Fargo had missed the almost silent whisper. Suddenly, a heavy blow fell on the back of his head, and the ground came roaring up to meet him and spun around crazily. He lashed out with his fist, spinning about, connected a glancing blow with his attacker, then staggered to his feet as he felt the man hit him again. He stayed on his feet, and a knife appeared out of the whirlpool, a long glittering knife blade that would slice through his neck.

He caught the hand that held it, forced himself back, bit his tongue hard to force his head to clarity, to force the world to stand still again as he wrestled with the Indian. Yes, Indian. His sight cleared again. An Indian virtually indistinguishable from the one staked on the ground, at least what he could see of him as they fought for the blade.

And strong, damn strong, powerful sinews and catlike reactions. Fargo held onto the man's hand that held the knife, then summoned his strength, poured it into his right hand as he forced it upward. He kicked out with his foot, connecting with the Indian's kneecap. The man staggered, was off balance for a mere second, just long enough for Fargo to throw him off his feet onto the ground. Fargo sat astride the man, forcing his hands down, beating his hand against a rock again and again until the Indian let go of the blade. With a powerful wrench, he flipped the Indian onto his belly and pulled his arms up hard behind him.

"You Havasupai?" Fargo asked. "Why kill man?" He knew only a few words in their language, which was unlike any of the other Indian tongues, and he hoped he was pronouncing the words intelligibly. But even so, the man under him didn't answer, so Fargo jerked his arms up again. The Indian grunted in pain, and Fargo repeated his questions again in the Havasupai tongue, then in English. Still no answer and he was beginning to wonder if maybe the Indian didn't understand. The staked Indian began to try to speak through the gag. Holding the pinioned man's arms with one hand, Fargo pulled the Arkansas toothpick from his ankle sheath. There was no rope within reach, and he couldn't take the risk of loosening his hold for a scant second. Within reach was one stake and a length of leather thong that held the other Indian's ankle. Fargo reached over and sliced a length of it, freeing the man's foot, then quickly tied the second man's hands. And tied 'em damn tight, too.

He stood and, with the point of his knife in the second Indian's back, got him to his feet. Fargo whistled, and in a moment the pinto appeared. Fargo retrieved thick rope from his saddle and bound the second Indian up tight, ankle and wrist, and propped him up against a rock. The Havasupai who'd attacked him was mad as a hornet, his black eyes spit fire. Fargo sliced the gag off the other's mouth. At first glance the two of them looked exactly the same, like twins, only the staked one wore a breechcloth and the other was in buckskin trousers, his chest bare and a few feathers woven into his long braids. But now that he had a chance to study their faces, he saw they weren't quite identical. The one that attacked him had narrower eyes, whereas the one staked to the ground stared back at him with two round dark eyes.

"Why kill man?" Fargo asked again. He knew the words weren't exactly what he wanted to say, but, hell, these two would get the idea. To his surprise the man staked on the ground began speaking in English.

"I am Taima. This is my brother, Inteus. Always

make trouble for our tribe. Never learn. Always make trouble."

As Taima spoke, Inteus sat listening with hate in his eyes. Taima's voice was rasping, and Fargo realized it was because of the rawhide band. He sliced it off Taima's neck, then secured his freed foot again. No use taking any chances.

"Long ago, when Inteus was a boy, old men make Jelka," Taima continued. "Make Jelka many times. But Inteus never learn."

"Jelka. What's that?"

"Old men make fire of dung, hold bad child's head in smoke long time. Almost die. Others make fun. Throw dung. Many times this Jelka, but Inteus never learn. Always make trouble." Fargo was unsure whether to believe Taima. He could be lying. There was no doubt the two were brothers. Beyond that, it was impossible to tell what was going on.

"Why is he killing you?"

"Many years ago, Inteus tried to hurt girl in tribe. Elders make him go out of the place of blue water. Make him to never come back. But this year some ghost make trouble in the village. Elders say it is spirit of Inteus returning. This spirit even leave footprints. I follow footprints for one moon. Then I find Inteus. We fight."

"What have you got to say?" Fargo asked Inteus. The Havasupai glared at him but would not speak.

"He can say nothing because I speak truth," Taima said.

"Maybe you don't speak English," Fargo said to Inteus.

The man's eyes flashed pure hate again, and he spoke at last.

"I speak white man speak."

"Your brother is telling truth?"

Inteus shrugged but wouldn't say more.

Fargo considered the situation. It was impossible to tell if Taima was lying or not. He didn't want to let either one of them go. But time was pressing. The midday sun had started to lower, though the day was still blasting hot. If he got back to the town of Nowhere by nightfall, at least he could put some solid steel handcuffs on these two until he found out the real story. And if he didn't make it back to town, he'd be spending a night out in the desert with the two of them sawing away on their ropes behind his back and ready to draw a knife on him and each other. In a moment he'd made up his mind.

"You're coming with me," Fargo said.

"Our horses are behind that rock," Taima said helpfully.

Fargo retrieved the knife he'd wrested from Inteus and stuck it in his belt. Then he left the two for a moment and went to retrieve the two palomino ponies. He turned when Taima shouted out to him and found that in the scant few minutes he'd been gone, Inteus had managed to roll over to a sharp-edged boulder and had almost succeeded in wearing through the ropes on his wrists. Fargo bound him again and had no doubt that if Taima had been able to, he'd have done the same.

It took him a half hour to get the two ponies tethered behind the pinto and the Havasupai up onto them, their hands bound tight behind them, wrists as well as elbows. It was damn painful, he knew, but much harder to work out of. And he wasn't taking any chances with either one of them now.

For the rest of the afternoon, he rode hard, kept the ponies moving along, kept an eye out behind him, stopping from time to time to check their ropes. The sun was just starting to set in a glory of fiery rose, and they were galloping in a line across a thick sage plain when Inteus made his move. Fargo felt a jolt on the rope that tethered the horses, and Taima cried out in incoherent alarm. Fargo looked back to see the last pony that Inteus had been on a moment before was riderless.

"I saw him. Back there in the sage!" Taima called excitedly, trying to gesture with his shoulders.

Fargo reined in and turned back. He doubted Inteus had got his hands free of the ropes. Nevertheless, the foolish Havasupai had simply thrown himself off his pony into the sage. Or was he so foolish? Fargo drew his Colt and rode at a walk slowly retracing their path to the point where he calculated that Inteus had fallen to the ground. His eye scanned the sage, searching for a movement, a flicker of something that didn't belong. Taima was looking intently, too, as they rode at a walk through the thick sage, crossing and recrossing the area. Fargo started from the center and made a spiral outward, his keen eyes searching the bushes. But even with his arms bound, Inteus had somehow managed to slither away through the sage. The light dimmed, and the first stars twinkled above. Taima had remained silent until they turned toward the town, and it was clear Fargo had given up the search.

"I must find the footprints of Inteus again," Taima said. "For my tribe, I must do this."

Fargo was inclined to believe Taima. But he kept him tied up anyway. He'd decide what to do when they got to Nowhere. It was nearly midnight when they clopped into town. Nowhere looked as deserted as before, though there were voices and laughter floating out of the Nowhere Saloon.

Fargo dismounted and tethered the three horses. He drew from his belt the knife he'd taken from Inteus and pulled Taima off the palomino.

"If I let you go free, what will you do?" Fargo asked.

"Go to find the footsteps of my brother."

There was no stopping him, apparently. It wasn't likely Taima would come after him. Fargo had saved his life, after all. Maybe Taima was telling the truth, maybe not. But now he realized that with Inteus gone, it was impossible to get to the bottom of it. Fargo sliced off the ropes. Without a pause Taima mounted.

"How are you called?" Taima asked as he was getting ready to ride out. When Fargo spoke his name, Taima nodded. "This name is in stories even so far as the shadow by the blue water. My people know you. We will be friends."

Taima raised his right hand gravely and then rode off. Fargo realized too late that the Havasupai had taken both palominos with him. He shook his head, tied the pinto near the trough, where it could drink its fill. Then he went inside the saloon.

Sims was carrying a tray of beer toward a table filled with laughing men. Fargo recognized a few of the faces, all locals. A rangy redhead seemed to be in the middle of telling a story. He pounded on the table.

"So what did you tell 'em, Zeke?" one of the men called out.

The redhead raised his fist to the ceiling and took a swig of beer.

"I says twenty-four dollars or nothing!" Zeke exclaimed. "I says you want six, you pay for six. At twenty-four dollars—"

"—Or nothing!" the rest of the men chimed in with a laugh.

Fargo wondered what was going on. He wandered over to the bar where Sims stood polishing a glass.

"Zeke made a killing today," Sims explained in answer to Fargo's quizzical look. "He's out his stock of useless canoes. All of 'em. We've been telling him it's crazy to have a bunch of boats in the middle of the desert, but—"

"Hold on," Fargo said. "Canoes? He sold 'em to who?"

"Why, Cavell Barnes and that bunch of no-goods came creeping back into town this afternoon. A bunch of us went out on the street with guns and said if they started cutting up, we was going to take some action. They said they'd just come to buy some boats. Heard we had some in Nowhere. Ain't that the damnedest thing? Behaved themselves just fine. And old Zeke got tip-top dollar for those stupid old wash buckets. So tonight, the whole town's here celebrating."

"What did Barnes want boats for?"

Sims stopped polishing the glass and blinked. "Don't know anybody asked him. Hey, Zeke! You hear Cavell Barnes say why they wanted your old bathtubs?"

"They didn't tell me straight out like," Zeke called back. "But I heard two of 'em talking about what they were going to do when they got their hands on all that gold."

"Gold?" another man called out. "There ain't no gold in these parts. Maybe they were going to float up to Colorado Territory."

"River runs the other direction, stupid," somebody said.

"I heard Barnes tell his men they were going down the Big Canyon," somebody else put in.

That confirmed Fargo's worst suspicions. Now Paulina would be completely crazy to go. He swore to himself and left hurriedly, heading for the hotel. The hotel proprietor was over at Zeke's party, and the lobby was deserted. Fargo climbed the steps and made his way down the dark hallway to Paulina's door. It was open a crack. With his hand on his Colt, he pushed it open. The room was deserted, the bed neatly made. The armoire stood open, and there were no clothes inside.

Paulina had gone, goddamn it. And he knew where. Stubborn as a mule, she'd headed out to shoot the killing rapids of the Colorado River. And now Cavell Barnes and his gang of bastards were going down the river, too. And if the white water didn't get her in its grip and chew her to pieces, then they would.

3

In a fury Fargo rushed back to the Nowhere Saloon, cursing himself, cursing Paulina and her crazy fixation.

"Sorry, I forgot to mention it," Sims said. "It was all Zeke's excitement made me forgetful. Sure, that lady writer bought a boat from Zeke—well, that was the day before Barnes and his men came and bought the rest of 'em—and she and that fellow named Bishy strapped that boat on a travois and rode out for the Grand Canyon just an hour after you left. That would have been yesterday morning." By the sudden stricken expression on Sims' face, Fargo realized that the bartender had belatedly put two and two together and got trouble.

"Right," Fargo said. "So now Paulina's heading down the river with that pack of bastards hot on her tail."

He wheeled around and left. As he swung onto the pinto, exhaustion settled on him. He'd had a long hard ride down to Dofield's ranch and another all the way back. And then there had been the strange encounter with the two Havasupai brothers, Inteus and Taima. The moon hung like a silver coin on the night's diamond–studded black velvet. But there was no time to stop for rest now. Paulina and Bishy had set out for the Grand Canyon with that boat packed on a travois and had been riding for two days. Even at a leisurely pace, unless they'd encountered trouble, they would have reached the shore of the Big Colorado River by now. He rode slowly out of town, concentrating on the ground, looking for any signs of their passing, thankful for the bright light of the moon just beginning to wane. The tracks in the ground were confusing, lots of horses, wagon ruts, places where the earth was too hard for footprints or too sandy, and so the wind had blown the prints away.

Half a mile out of town, alongside the hard-packed trail, he found what he'd been looking for—the clear impression of two deep marks, the poles of a single travois. He'd reasoned that Paulina and Bishy would follow the line of the Little Colorado River northward and launch their boat from where those two rivers met. And Cavell Barnes and his gang of ruffians were right behind her thinking they were going to find gold. He kept his eye out for signs of other travois, but didn't see any—maybe Barnes and his gang had set out due west, planning to launch farther down on the river. And maybe they were after Paulina, too. Fargo wondered where they'd got such a crazy idea about the gold. Ore was always found in quartz deposits, and he hadn't seen any quartz in this part of the country ever. The idea of finding gold around here was ridiculous.

The pinto was tired. He could tell by the way it took the hills, resolutely but less effortlessly than usual. It valiantly pushed on through the long night as if sensing the need for top speed and at times he held it back, reined it in for water, for rest. On and on he went, passing through the empty moonlit land with its fantastical rock formations, the Ovaro's hooves slicing the dry cracked earth.

Despite the waves of tiredness that swept over him throughout the long night, he forced himself to stay alert. He avoided riding near rock outcroppings and cliffs where he could be ambushed. And, over and over again, his keen eyes swept the landscape, searching for the glow of a campfire's embers. He sniffed the cold night air for any trace of wood smoke from a campfire.

Cavell Barnes and his men were out there somewhere. Paulina and Bishy might be, too, unless they'd already made it to the river. And then there were the two Havasupai. No telling where they'd got to. He didn't fancy another ambush and wrestling match with Inteus.

A peach dawn streaked the sky and lit the tops of the distant buttes. As the hours passed, his concern for the Ovaro grew. It had been three days of hard riding, galloping hour after hour across rough terrain. At this pace another horse would have gone short already, have been crippled. But the powerful pinto kept going. Nevertheless, he could feel the horse was bone-tired. It was at just such a time that the mount could make a misstep into a prairie dog hole or misjudge a rocky slope and snap a leg. Despite his hurry, he slowed the pinto down, made it walk for a few miles before giving it free rein again.

The day turned hot with a bleached sky that promised no rain. It was late afternoon already when he spotted the mighty Colorado in the wide gap between two buttes where the rivers met. Slices of crumbling talus and towering striped canyon walls came into view. The land around was sere and stark with small tufts of dry yellow grass and prickly pear cactus. As if it knew the goal was in sight, the Ovaro poured on the speed, galloping all out in a froth, flecks of sweat flying in the air. Again, Fargo had to hold back the eager pinto.

He paused on a high embankment above the meeting of the rivers. Below snaked the turbid muddy waters of the Big Colorado River and the turquoise-tinted Little Colorado poured into it like a colorful feather plume. The canyon cut narrow here where the rivers met. He scoured the scene, looking for any sign, hoping to spot Paulina's familiar figure along with Bishy. There was no one in sight.

But a black circle, a fire pit, marred the muddy bank below. The Ovaro plunged down the slope to the river. Fargo dismounted and knelt, waved his hand over the gray ashes. A little heat. He moved his hand closer to make sure it wasn't just the sun, and then he was sure. The fire had snuffed out about dawn. Something gleamed on the ground nearby. A broken pen nib, like the one he'd seen Paulina writing with.

Twenty yards downstream, he found the parallel tracks of the travois, then the abandoned poles and harnesses, two saddles and bridles piled neatly beside a rock. They'd abandoned their equipment and let the horses run wild. He wondered what in hell Paulina had planned to do at journey's end. She struck him as the kind of woman who didn't plan ahead, but just trusted to luck.

At water's edge he saw the wide-scraped path where the flat-bottomed boat had been launched into the water. In the mud were etched two sets of prints unmistakably belonging to Paulina and Bishy. He'd missed them by half a day.

He peered downstream where the milky brown river turned from a southwest direction to a due west course, winding between the disintegrating cliffs of yellow, white, and orange. There was no way to catch them now except by boat. There was no trail downriver, since the cliffs rose time and again straight up out of the roiling water. He needed a canoe. And somebody to look after the Ovaro. He had a sudden inspiration and mounted the pinto. He rode up and out of the canyon, then turned to ride along the lip of the canyon, west toward the sinking sun and the Circle D Ranch.

Hours later, as he rode through the piñons out under the stars, he spotted a red glow up ahead, a strange pinkish smudge on the horizon. The pinto nickered nervously. At first he thought it was a glimmer of the sunset remaining in the sky, but it was an hour too late. The smell of smoke reached him, and the pinto sprang forward.

He burst out of the trees into the meadow at the Circle D Ranch. The compound was burning, roaring orange and yellow flames licking the black sky, spraying sparks like ruby comets. A rising column of smoke obliterated the stars. Dark figures—he recognized some of Dofield's hands—dashed back and forth from the one small well, trying to douse the flames with buckets of water. The fire had already been burning for some time, he could see. One of the larger buildings, the ranch house was already burned out, nothing but an empty shell of blackened timbers. The bunkhouse, which stood somewhat apart, was intact, but the barn was burning. It sent showers of sparks upward that fell down on the wood shingle roof of one of the storehouses.

In an instant Fargo was galloping across the meadow to help out. As the sound of the approaching horse reached them over the roar of the fire, Fargo was shocked to see the ranch hands throw down their buckets and grab their rifles. A warning shot whizzed overhead. Fargo raised his hands high above his head as the Ovaro cantered in and came to a stop. Then in the flickering glow of the flames, the ranch hands apparently recognized him.

"What the hell's going on?" Fargo shouted above the roar of the fire. He got down and slapped the pinto away from the dancing flames as one of the hands shouted out to Ed Dofield. The hands returned to fighting the fire. The rancher appeared at the door of the bunkhouse and hobbled forward, dragging his right foot and using a rifle as a crutch. His face was drawn and haggard.

"Those men you warned me about," Ed Dofield said without preamble, "came in this afternoon. Two of 'em at first, just materialized at the door of the ranch house. They looked all right. Harriet—" His voice choked, and he looked into the fire for a long moment. "She let 'em in, like she always does strangers. Hid all that money first, but they somehow saw her doing it. Before we knew what was happening, that whole gang was in here. Crazy, plumb crazy like they were drunk, mean drunk. Shit—" He paused again, and Fargo saw tears of rage in the man's eyes. "Ran off the horses, just for the hell of it. Shot three of my ranch hands, they were just boys mind you, just boys. My wife, she—" His voice broke, and his face turned to chiseled stone. "She's in the bunkhouse, don't want to see nobody."

"Bastards," Fargo said under his breath.

"Just like you said, that short gray-haired fellow named Barnes was leading 'em." Dofield's voice was cold, deadly cold. "And there was that big fellow they called Platan. Got his arm in a sling. And they had some Indian with 'em, too, a Havasupai by the look of him. Big one, too, strong. Goddamn it. I always thought those Havasupai were peaceable like." Dofield picked up his rifle and shook it as if he could jolt it into pieces. "But I swear, the next redskin I see I'm going to blast his fucking head off."

"The rest of 'em were white," Fargo pointed out. "You gonna shoot the next dozen white men you see, too?"

"Shit," Dofield said. "You're right about that. Son of a bitch!" He limped away in the direction of the bunkhouse, leaving a trail of blood. He'd got shot in the leg, but he wasn't even feeling it.

Fargo gritted his teeth for a moment. So one of the Havasupai had joined up with Barnes. Instinct told him it was Inteus. And they'd robbed Ed Dofield of thousands of dollars, raped his wife, shot some hands, tried to burn him out. Which direction had they gone now? Dofield hadn't said anything about seeing any canoes. He pushed away the thought of what might happen if they got their hands on Paulina.

There was nothing to do with his rage but work it out. Fargo looked about for a bucket and saw none. But an old shovel had been tossed on the ground by the bunkhouse. He seized it and began shoveling dirt onto the fire, dashing in as close as he dared to the raging flames as the intense heat curled the hairs on his arms and scorched his skin. He helped the others draw water out of the well, pass it along in a line, and dash it sizzling onto the flames. Several times Dofield appeared and tried to help, but the younger men sent him away to tend to his wife and his bullet wound. Fargo climbed up onto the roof of the storehouses and stamped out the little flames as they took root there.

A few hours later, the fire was finally put out. Dawn was still hours away. Fargo and the hands hauled a last round of water to wash the soot off their faces and hands. Fargo got a chance to ask if Barnes and his men had canoes with them, and the hands confirmed they'd seen the boats tied to travois harnessed onto their horses. So Barnes was probably still planning to head for the river.

It was a couple of hours before dawn. Dofield appeared. His leg was bandaged now, and he hobbled with the aid of a cane. He was carrying blankets for the four ranch hands so they could bed down in one of the storehouses. They each took one and then stood around their boss expectantly, as if unwilling to leave him alone.

Fargo stood beside Dofield as the rancher surveyed the disaster. The acrid smoke stung their nostrils. The barn was nothing but an empty cage of blackened timbers lit by the last flush of dying embers. Just then the roof beam gave way, collapsed with an earsplitting crash, sending up fountains of red sparks and clouds of ash and smoke.

"Still got the storehouses and the bunkhouse," Dofield said. He spoke as if sleepwalking. "We'll be all right, boys. Tomorrow we'll round up the horses. Still got the sheep. And it don't matter about that money anyway. There ain't many men can say they were rich, even if it was only for one day. My only regret is I didn't pay out that bonus to you boys yesterday so you'd have taken your money and hid it in your bunks."

The men were silent. Fargo's head was spinning.

He'd missed two nights' sleep and was past the point of exhaustion. But it was time to get help. He had to get a canoe, get down to the canyon to find Paulina. Before Cavell Barnes and his crew did.

"Guess there ain't no justice in the world," Ed Dofield said quietly.

"You *make* your justice," Fargo said. "And that's just what I aim to do. I'll get Barnes and the rest of them. And we even got some luck with us, because that one didn't burn down," he said, pointing to the storehouse where he'd seen the boat. Ed Dofield looked confused.

Then Fargo explained all that had happened when he returned to Nowhere and why he'd come back to the Circle D, that he needed that old flat-bottomed boat fixed up and fast, made ready for river travel. The men listened, disbelieving at first, then nodding eagerly as they understood his plan.

He needed tin nailed onto the hull, he told them, and animal stomachs—sheep stomachs were fine—inflated and tucked in the bow and stern. He needed the boat packed with extra rowlocks, sockets, pins, patches of sheet tin, additional animal stomachs, and food supplies. He had to have a watertight box of some kind big enough for pistols and ammunition. And he needed a canvas cover nailed over the top in front and back to keep her from swamping, leaving just enough room toward the center for two people.

"*Two* people?" Dofield asked. "Hell, we'll all come with you to get those bastards."

"That boat can only take two men over the rapids."

"Then, I'll go," Dofield said.

"No. You stay here with your ranch and your missus," Fargo said. All four hands volunteered immediately and he chose a dark-haired serious fellow named Billy, who looked sturdy and strong.

"There's a steep trail down to the river just two miles from here," Dofield said. "It switchbacks into a side canyon and down to the water's edge. My guess is that's the way those bastards went."

Fargo considered his dilemma. If he rode all the way back upstream to where the two rivers converged, to the spot where Paulina launched, he would lose valuable time catching up to her and to Barnes. On the other hand, if she and Bishy had come to grief right away, before they made it this far downstream, he might miss seeing them. Or what was left of them. Of course, if the rapids got them right away, he reasoned, there was nothing he could do about it. In a moment he'd made up his mind.

"In the morning, we'll follow Barnes' tracks. See where they lead us."

"All right, we'll get right to fixing up this boat and have it ready to go at dawn," Dofield said, patting him on the shoulder. "Meanwhile, you get some sleep, Fargo. You gotta hunt down those—those—" Dofield seemed unable to say more and limped toward the storehouse.

The ranch hands all offered their blankets to him, and he made his way to another of the storehouses.

There, he fell asleep on a pile of bearskins and knew no more until he felt a hand on his shoulder. Ed Dofield bent over him.

Outside, the hands had a campfire going, and over the acrid odor of smoke and char, he smelled coffee. He dashed cold well water on his face and saw he'd overslept. The sun had been up two hours already, but he guessed he'd needed the rest. After a tin mug of strong coffee and a hurried meal of smoked bacon and eggs, he felt better than he had in days.

Some of the Circle D horses had already wandered back in, and the ranch hands had four of them saddled. A travois was attached to the fifth on which was loaded the boat. Fargo inspected it and saw that everything he'd asked had been done. And more. They'd gone overboard on the hull, nailing tin double and triple thick at the bow and stern and along the sides. It looked indestructible, but Fargo knew the power of the water could tear up any boat if you weren't lucky. There seemed to be plenty of food supplies packed inside.

Fargo felt a soft warm breath on his neck and a hairy muzzle. He reached up to pat the pinto.

"I'll take good care of that Ovaro," Ed Dofield said. "Though, from the looks of it, that horse could use a good rest." The rancher staggered to his horse and two of the hands helped him mount. Fargo knew the pinto would be well-cared for. He'd seen how wisely Ed Dofield and his hands treated their livestock.

Fargo and Billy got onto the readied horses, and

the other ranch hand mounted, holding a tether to lead the horse with the travois. The other two hands would stay behind with Mrs. Dofield, who had remained hidden in the bunkhouse. As they started away from the ranch, Fargo heard the pinto whinny. He saw a flicker of movement at the window of the bunkhouse. He waved back at her, knowing she was watching, and wanting to tell her in the only way he could that he'd hunt down those men if it was the last thing he did. Then they were lost among the piñons, heading down the trail. They followed the thick travois tracks that turned, as Ed Dofield thought they might, immediately down toward the river.

It took four hours to descend the rocky canyon. The switchbacks bent like hairpins down the steep canyon walls. They dismounted often to lead the horses and lift the heavy travois when it became stuck. As they descended, they spotted the gang's abandoned horses below, still saddled, standing crowded onto the narrow embankment beside the silty river. When they came closer, Fargo saw that the horses had been hobbled, too. Instead of letting them run free, the gang had tied their forelegs, cruelly, insuring that the animals would starve to death or collapse of thirst. The ranch hands freed the horses, who immediately walked down to the river to drink. They'd take them back to the Circle D. They backed up the travois to the river and slid the boat in.

It was a sturdy craft, Fargo saw with relief as it bobbed up and down in the water. He and the boy named Billy were just about to get inside and launch when a voice called out. A figure, an Indian in buckskins appeared among the rocks. For a moment Fargo thought it was Inteus because of his garb, but then he recognized the round dark eyes, Taima hurrying toward him.

The reaction of Ed Dofield and the two ranch hands was instantaneous. Without hesitation, they drew and began to fire. Taima stopped, surprised, then hit the ground and crawled behind a rock. Fargo threw himself forward of them to get their attention and shouted for them to stop shooting.

"It's that Havasupai son of a bitch!" Ed Dofield screamed, shaking with rage. "Shoot the hell out of him. Now!"

Fargo quickly explained how alike the two brothers looked and how certain he was that they had encountered Inteus, the other brother. Doubtful, they lowered their guns. Fargo held up his hand and walked toward the rock where Taima was hiding. Just before he reached the rock, he spoke.

"They thought you were Inteus. Your brother attacked them last night." There was no answer from Taima. Fargo continued walking until Taima came into sight, crouched behind the rock, knife in hand. A bullet had grazed his arm, but otherwise, he was unhurt. He did not stand up but continued to hide behind the rock.

"I track Inteus," Taima said, speaking in English. "I see him fighting and burning white man's place. Then I see him leaving to go to water. I hurry ahead. I wait to ambush and kill him. But no chance. He is with so many pale men. They go in canoes and take Inteus with them. The river god will kill them all. Now I wait here to see the spirit of my brother floating on the water. Then I know he is dead."

Fargo remembered that the Havasupai, even though they lived by the river in the Grand Canyon, rarely traveled by canoe. Instead, they came and went from their canyon village by climbing up to the rim and going by horseback across the high desert.

"The river god might not kill them all," Fargo said. "I am going after them. You come with me." Behind him, Fargo could feel Ed Dofield and his boys waiting, still suspicious of the Indian.

Taima glanced their direction then out at the river, considering. Fargo read fear there in Taima's expression. The Havasupai knew the river's force firsthand, and had a respectful awe of it. But in the Indian's face he read another kind of fear, one he could not so easily decode.

"Yes, I come with Fargo," Taima said. "Yes, I come to find my brother even though this will make the river god angry. Yes, I come."

Taima glanced nervously back at Ed Dofield and his hands, clearly afraid they would begin firing again. Fargo returned to them and explained. Billy looked both disappointed and relieved that he would not be accompanying Fargo on this dangerous journey. Ed and his boys put their guns away. Once assured of safety, Taima ventured forth and seated himself in the boat.

Fargo eased himself into the forward seat. There was just enough room for the two of them in the center of the craft. The bow and stern were filled with flotation sheep stomachs, the rest packed with supplies and covered over by canvas. Fargo leaned left and right and saw that although the boat rocked, the tin-sheathed flat bottom kept it fairly steady. Fargo showed Taima how to pull the canvas tight so the least amount of water could get inside. Even so, they would have to bail out water when the going got rough. And it was going to get very rough. Fargo had had some experience with boating in broken water, but nobody had ever tried the raging Colorado River before and lived to tell about it.

Fargo grasped the oars and glanced out at the great Colorado River. He hoped he was making the right decision, he hoped Paulina had at least made it past this point and he had some chance of finding her further downstream. The river was relatively wide and quiet here, the milky brown water hardly broken by rocks. But he knew what lay ahead.

Ed Dofield and his boys shoved them off from shore and stood waving as Fargo pushed with the oars to propel them out into midstream. Dofield opened his mouth to shout something but then thought better of it. Fargo knew what the man had been about to say. The insistent current caught them, and he pushed the nose around until they were headed downstream. They shot forward with a backward wave at the Circle D men, who soon disappeared from view around a bend.

High above them the gargantuan ruddy rocks were rounded like elephant backs. Bits of bunch grass and trailing wild roses grew in the cracks of the cliffs. Where there was a sandy bank, bright green serviceberry and squaw-berry bushes grew thickly. The sky was a pale blue ribbon high above them as they darted from the shadow of one deep cliff into sparkling sunlight and back into shadow.

Steering the boat was pretty much a one-man job, he realized. But they also had to keep a lookout for Barnes and Inteus as well as for any signs of Paulina and Bishy. Fargo told Taima that keeping a watch would be his job, while Fargo would steer. If Taima spotted anything, he was to open the water-proof box that was tied down on the floor of the boat between them, hand Fargo his Colt, and arm himself with one of the other loaded pistols. As they floated downstream, they practiced it again and again until Taima could do it quickly. They kept practicing until it became second nature. Between these drills, Taima sat upright in the boat, looking downstream, his round eyes searching the river and the rocky banks.

An hour later, Fargo knew they were approaching the first rapid. It was the sound that told him. Above the steady whispering rush of the water came a sullen boom echoing just ahead, accompanied by a sudden hurrying increase in the speed of the current. Whirlpools and eddies downstream of the rocks began to spin faster, the river narrowed and tumbled, the sound of the boom grew louder moment by moment.

As they rounded a curve, Fargo saw ahead a long stretch of broken water, twisted and churning. He aimed the boat down a smooth-surfaced sluice, and it glided down. Then, when the boat paused in the whirlpool just below, he dipped the paddle and held the boat there, stalled and unmoving. He handed off the paddles to Taima and mimed what to do to hold the boat in position. Then he raised himself up a foot or two in a half crouch while he reconnoitered the rapids below, plotting how they were going to navigate it, looking for the deepest and smoothest channels. It wasn't a bad one, this first rapids, but it had been awhile since he'd fought a wild river. It would get plenty wilder, and he wanted to learn everything the river had to teach him before he had to go up against its full strength.

Finally, he sat down again and took the oars from Taima, propelling the boat forward. They shot like an arrow along a path of glassy water between riffles, heading for a boulder the size of a buffalo. On either side of the huge rock the water plummeted downward in a white foaming curl. Taima muffled a cry as they headed straight toward the rock, and at the last moment Fargo dipped his left oar to aim the boat straight down the smooth V. The boat dropped several feet with a stomach-gripping plunge and seemed to dive under. The freezing cold water poured in over them, and they were instantly soaked to the bone. All around was the roaring, a loud shout of water dashed against the rocks, and for a moment it seemed as if they would sink, but their boat bobbed up and floated downstream.

"Start bailing!" Fargo called out to Taima. It was a good thing they had the canvas covers and the flotations. Otherwise they'd have already been swamped. But there was no time to think. Before him was a line of sharp rocks like the lower jaw of a monstrous animal. Fargo aimed for the largest opening, and once again the boat dropped a yard, the water poured in. After the little hesitation and a paddle prod from Fargo, they continued downstream. Taima was bailing like mad as, again and again, Fargo aimed for that glassy V that was the safe chute between the rocks and battled the big back wave that crested just downstream of large rocks. After a few more minutes, the roaring of the water diminished somewhat and the river calmed.

They'd run the first rapid, and they'd been lucky. It hadn't been a rough one, and he'd had a chance to get some practice. But he knew there was much worse to come. Taima finished bailing out, and then gave his full attention to his job as lookout. They floated, drying out in the sun, as Fargo propelled the boat to keep the keel where the current ran fastest and deepest. Solid red rock cliffs rose high above, here and there chiseled into graceful arches and shadowy caves filled with still water. Limpid pools were edged with green fringes of wild cherry. The late afternoon shadows were already gathering.

"Tell me about your brother," Fargo said, resting the oars. "Why is he with Cavell Barnes and his gang?"

"This I do not know," Taima said. "After I left you in the white village, I went to search for footprints of Inteus. Soon I find his track and see him join up with many white men. I see him talking to them in white man speak. And then they get very excited."

"Your brother is pretty slippery," Fargo said, and then had to explain to Taima what he meant by that.

"Since he was a boy, he is able to disappear. He walks like a shadow, and it is very hard to track him. I am the best tracker in Havasu and still he is better."

"Your people exiled him, isn't that right?" Fargo asked.

"Yes, sent him out of village never to come back. But we know he is always sneaking back now to make trouble."

Fargo asked Taima to tell him about the Havasu village, which lay a few days travel downriver. Though he'd never been there, Fargo knew that the village was in a paradisal side canyon to the south of the Grand Canyon and high above it. Taima told him the village was accessible only by a trail that led down from the southern canyon rim, although Fargo had heard a rumor there was a secret underground passage of some kind that also gave access to the desert rim above.

"And what about from below?" Fargo asked. "Is there a path down to the Big Canyon?"

"Through our village runs beautiful blue water," Taima said. This is the meaning of Ha-va-su-pai . . . water, blue, people. The blue water goes down to join this great river down below. It goes down, very very far down." Fargo knew he was talking about a gigantic waterfall. "Here no one can go. Havasupai do not go down to the great river below but stay high up in the village of blue water."

"There's *no* path down into the Grand Canyon?" Fargo asked.

"No," Taima said. There was something in the tone of his voice that made Fargo suspect he was lying. And if his suspicions were correct and there was a path, it was an entrance undoubtedly known only to the tribe, and they would want to keep it a secret. But Inteus would know about it. And here he was bringing a dozen no-goods right to his tribe's secret back door. The thought had probably occurred to Taima, too.

"You know anything about gold in this canyon?"

"That yellow metal that makes white men crazy? No. I never hear of gold here." This time Fargo sensed Taima was telling the truth. They were quiet for a while, letting the river carry them. The river narrowed, and they shot through another rapids, not quite as challenging as the first. And then they were floating again.

"So many white people on this river," Taima said when they had time to talk again.

"So many? What are you talking about?" Fargo asked.

"I saw another boat. Before my brother and the white men came to the river. I was waiting to ambush him. And when they were coming down the slope, I saw a boat with two white people. Out on the river. And strange thing—"

"A woman?"

"Squaw, yes. Much surprise. Hair like corn silk."

"Those are the people I'm looking for," Fargo said, relieved that Paulina and Bishy had made it that far at least.

"You are looking for squaw?" Taima laughed. "Aha! Looking for squaw? Not for evil men?"

"Them, too," Fargo said with a laugh at Taima's joke. Then he subsided into thought. So Paulina and Bishy were downstream of Cavell Barnes and his men by only a short distance. And, according to Fargo's calculations, Barnes had launched only a few hours ahead of them. He realized they'd have to take some drastic action. They'd have to catch up to Barnes and then somehow slip past him to find Paulina and Bishy farther downstream. If Barnes and his men hadn't caught them yet.

"The white men are looking for this squaw, too," Taima said then, interrupting his thoughts.

"What?" He came out of his thoughts. "Why do you say that?"

"Because when the squaw goes by, the other white men are coming down path to river. They see and they yell and scream, shoot guns. She waves to them. Like this." Taima stopped speaking and did an imitation of Paulina waving gaily. "Then they hurry to get into boats. So they look for squaw, too. Hair like cornsilk. Very surprise."

Hell, that made things more complicated, Fargo realized. Barnes and his men spotted Paulina floating by, helpless as a duck. He could bet they were traveling as fast as they could to get their grimy hands on her. Despite the gravity of the situation, he smiled to himself as he imagined Paulina waving at them as her boat carried her swiftly downstream. She really was a crazy woman. But how the hell were Paulina and Bishy making out in these rapids? And how would they survive the more dangerous ones to come?

As if the river read his mind, he was brought out of his reverie by the sound of rapids ahead. Only this time, instead of the steady sullen boom he'd heard before, he heard also a clattery sound like an army of muskets firing. He knew that sound. It was the sound that thousands of tons of water made when dashed at high speeds against rocks and boulders, when it broke into foaming white crests and tumbled over and over, spiraling into whirlpools. It was the sound of a really bad rapid.

But, distracted by his thoughts, he'd heard it too late. The current had seized them. He gripped the oars tighter and aimed for the chutes, dropping the boat again and again into the thick white torrents. The cliffs seemed to fly by on either side. They rounded a bend and this time by the time he saw what was ahead, there was no way to stop the boat.

Suddenly, they were over the precipice, falling,

the bow driving straight downward into the raging white waves, the stern lifted up into the air, tons of cold water pouring in on top of them, shaking the boat like a toy.

The bow scraped against rocks, and the oars were torn from his hands as the powerful flow spun the boat about dizzyingly. Then they were being carried sideways, straight toward a jagged rock with such force that Fargo knew the boat would be split clean in half.

4

The white water raged all around them, as the boat hurtled sideways toward the jagged rock that would tear it asunder, splinter it into matchsticks. Taima was bailing, but it was almost futile. The boat was riding low. Fargo fumbled to grasp the left oar, throwing himself to the side as the water-filled boat rocked and more water poured in. Finally, he grabbed it, swung it out just as the boat was nearly there, then jammed it hard downward under the rock like a pivot. The river tried to wrench the oar from his grasp but he held fast. The pin of the rowlock lifted out of the socket, and the wooden oar groaned under the strain. An instant later the current caught the bow of the boat, spun it downstream, and they shot past the jagged rock, down a smooth chute.

"Keep bailing!" Fargo shouted to Taima. There were still some nasty rapids ahead. The boat was waterlogged but afloat. The flat bottom scraped against rocks submerged in the water. Fargo steered through several more chutes then heard the high crackling sound up ahead. He stalled the boat on a patch of backwater, just downstream of a big rock, and took a look ahead. Taima continued throwing the pails of water over the side.

It was bad ahead, narrow and steep with sharp rocks and precipitous descents that disappeared from his view. A fine mist rose up, a sign the white water was particularly violent. The broken water reflected flecks of late afternoon gold from sunrays streaming through the high clouds above. It was time to call it a day, Fargo realized. They'd have to pull over and try to figure out how to get past the next bad patch of white water. A few yards downstream was a narrow muddy bank that would make a lousy place to camp, but they had no choice. At least there was a pile of driftwood there to make a campfire. He propelled across to it, and he and Taima got out, then dragged the boat up onto the bank.

"Let's get a fire going and dry out," Fargo said, leaning down to unpack the supplies. Suddenly, out of the corner of his eye, he caught a movement. He glanced downstream where, across the river and two hundred yards farther down, he saw several men standing on the bank, barely visible around the edge of a rock cliff. He ducked down abruptly behind the beached boat and told Taima to get down, too. If they hadn't yet been spotted, any more movement might attract attention. He peered out, watching them.

"The white men see us?" Taima asked.

"Not yet."

"I think their boat is stuck in the river."

Yeah, that's what it looked like. The men continued to shout and gesticulate from onshore, looking the other way, downstream. They were too far away and the rapids too loud for him to make out any words. There were three of them. He recognized the big one, the man called Platan Arnez was there. He was glad to see the man's arm in a sling from the bullet he'd put in his arm back in the town of Nowhere.

They'd caught up to Barnes and his men and had been damn lucky not to have rounded a curve and run smack into them unaware. Now if they could just keep from being noticed. Large rocks hid most of the stern of their boat from the view of the men, but not the bow drawn up on shore. Moving very slowly, Fargo and Taima dragged a huge wad of tangled branches inch by inch down the bank, and positioned it alongside the beached bow to camouflage its shape.

Night came on early at the bottom of the Grand Canyon, the river and the cliffs were already swathed in shadows even though the sky overhead was still bright. They discovered that by crawling up the bank to the very foot of the cliff, they could get completely out of sight of the men farther downstream, yet keep an eye on them if they wanted by ducking back down behind the boat. And night would soon hide them completely.

There'd be no fire, Fargo thought with regret. He and Taima wrung out their clothes and spread them on the rocks, opened the waterproof canvas bag—well, almost waterproof—and retrieved drier clothes, then wrapped themselves in a couple of blankets. He realized he was ravenously hungry. They hadn't eaten since breakfast. On top of the food supplies was a large canvas envelope with a note pinned on it. Even though the note had been soaked and the running ink dyed the paper pale gray, he could read the traces of the words.

"Eat this first or it will spoil."

He knew Mrs. Dofield had packed it herself. Inside they found a dozen hard-boiled eggs, a pile of cold mutton slices, a paper bag of biscuits and a peach pie wrapped in waxy paper that had been squashed flat. Water had seeped in and spoiled the biscuits, but everything else tasted mighty fine. They ate as much as they could hold, then sat hunched against the cliff, wrapped in their blankets as the night came on.

The dusk turned blue. The men downstream lit a big bonfire of driftwood and the orange light flickered on the rocks. Fargo crept down to the boat and was surprised to see more men had appeared on the bank. As they moved around the campfire, their shadows, like dark giants, danced on the smooth cliff behind them. He counted ten, spotted Clive Barnes with them. There were four canoes pulled up on shore as well.

He guessed that somehow the group had got separated. The three men he'd seen before might have lost their boat, and the others must have landed once they reached the calmer waters below the rapids on the far shore and then had found a way to ford across. He looked in vain for Paulina, even wading out into the dark rushing water to get a better view of their firelit camp, but he couldn't spot her or Bishy or anybody tied up on the ground, either. She must be somewhere farther downstream. If she was still in one piece.

He had to find a way to get past them and locate Paulina. And night gave them the best chance to do it. He waded farther downstream in the darkness, holding onto rocks so as not to lose his footing. The water was icy, and a stiff wind blew. After a short distance, he came to a sandy shore and a shallow calm pool alongside the raging rapid. The rushing water shone white in the darkness as it plummeted over the rocks, the waves crashing with a thousand voices, while just downstream of it, the water calmed and spread out. An orange reflection of the distant campfire skipped up and down on the waves.

There was no way to shoot these rapids at night, Fargo decided. In broad daylight it might have been possible, although most sane men would choose to portage, to carry their boats around the rapids and launch again from down below. It looked as though Barnes and his gang had lost one of their boats because of this wild water. He scanned the banks, measured the still pool by the sandy shoal, saw that from here they could slip into the river below the white water and glide right by Barnes' campsite. Yes, they'd portage in dark of night, he decided, and he returned to where Taima waited.

For the next three hours, under the cover of darkness, they made numerous trips down to the small sandy beach unloading the boat and carrying the supplies and equipment parcel by parcel and piled it on the shore. With the campfire in their eyes and the moonlight unable to penetrate the deep canyon, Barnes and his men could not see them moving back and forth on the upstream opposite shore. Finally, the boat empty, they lifted it and sometimes floated it in the rocky and shallow water near the shore, making their headway inch by inch. It took an hour of effort before the empty boat was floating in the shallow pool and they began loading it again.

Fargo was glad to have the opportunity to assess what supplies Ed Dofield and his boys had packed in the boat. They had followed his instructions exactly. There were extra sheep stomachs, cured, stitched, and sealed with bear grease. When inflated and tied shut, they made good flotations in case the ones fore and aft began to leak. There was plenty of good trail food—mutton jerky, hardtack biscuits, and dried fruit, as well as packets of coffee and a tin pot and mugs. They'd also included extra tin for patches, a pair of oars, and other repair supplies.

When everything was back in the boat, it was riding low, the flat keel barely able to clear the bottom of the shallow pool. It was well after midnight now. At the camp, the fire had burned down to a dull glow of red embers, and sleeping forms lay all around like rocks.

He and Taima pushed the boat off into the water, all the way to the end of the shallow pool, then got aboard. Fargo grasped the oars and pushed off into the current. The boat was pulled out into the stream, and it moved off. Fargo peered into the darkness. He had good vision at night, and yet it was almost impossible to see. The water barely glimmered with the reflection of the starlight. But just ahead, as the river bent westward, the canyon walls opened up, moonlight fell across the water, and it seemed as bright as day.

In the shadow of the cliff, they floated silently past the sleeping camp. Taima held both pistols in hand just in case. Fargo bent his attention on the river. He could make no mistake just now. The water was gentle and undulated over the rocky bed. Several times he had to swerve to avoid protruding boulders, but in moments they had passed the camp.

Fargo breathed a sigh of relief as they floated out of the shadows and into the silvery flood of moonlight. Suddenly, there came a shout from the direction of the camp, now just behind them. Hell, they'd been spotted! Fargo glanced back over his shoulder but now with the moon hanging up above the lip of the canyon and dazzling his eyes, he could see nothing but blackness. A shot rang out and a bullet thudded into the side of the boat, the impact tipping it sideways.

"Get down!" Fargo shouted at Taima as more bullets whizzed overhead. "They're smarter than I thought. Posted a lookout."

"It's my brother," Taima said grimly. "Inteus never sleeps. And he sees in the dark."

There was no point in trying to return fire, since

they couldn't see what they were shooting at. Above the roar of the water, he could hear the men calling to one another. There were more shots, bullets zinging by furiously. And then the river turned, and they heard nothing but the roar of the water. Fargo sat up again and quickly corrected the sideways drift of the boat.

"They will follow?" Taima asked.

"I'm willing to bet they do," Fargo said. Of course, whoever had spotted them passing couldn't have seen who they were. But Barnes and his men were just the kind to come after them anyway.

The canyon walls widened here, falling back into dim and distant pagodas of high rock, opening up the sky above. The moon rose higher and flooded the canyon with its cold light.

Now Fargo bent all his attention to making good time, to putting as much distance between them and possible pursuit. He scanned the gleaming water ahead, aiming for the deepest fastest channels, sliding through the openings between the large rocks, pushing off impatiently to keep moving swiftly downstream. They had gone twenty minutes when he heard the sound of another rapid ahead—that deep booming and the musket-like clatter again, the telltale sound of dangerous white water. But this time he had no choice but to keep going. If they stopped again to portage, Barnes and his men were sure to catch up to them.

The water pulled them along faster and faster toward the rapids. A tumble of gigantic boulders lay across their path, and the boat darted in and out among them, scraping sometimes against the sides as the water threatened to swamp them, but always at the last possible second, tumbling free to plummet down the foaming chute and bob up for a moment before hurtling on. Fargo lost all sense of time as he battled the raging torrents, now in the bright white of the moonlight, now in the dark cliff shadows, using the oars now as a fulcrum, then as a paddle or to push off from a shoal or boulder. Taima silently bailed out the water that sloshed around in the boat as it filled again and again. It had just seemed that the rapids would never end when they rounded a bend and were plunged into the shadow of a towering cliff that momentarily hid the bright moon.

For a moment the darkness was blinding, and then Fargo saw a huge boulder dead in their path. The boat struck it a glancing blow, tilted, and plunged downward, falling, scraping against the rocks, the wood shattering at the impact. He lost his grip on the right oar as the water poured in around them, waves threatening to drown them. Still the boat dropped, scraping and bumping, he heard the wood splintering. The bow tilted forward, and it seemed they were dropping in a straight vertical. He held onto the gunwale, gasped for air, and heard Taima cry out. The boat tilted, overturned in the foaming water. He felt himself lifted, thrown out of the boat, dashed against a rock.

He gasped for air again, tried not to struggle as the current took him like a piece of driftwood, dragging him across the rocky bottom. He was floating downward, the current swallowing him. Waves battered him again and again. He came up for air and dashed the water from his eyes. He'd floated out into the moonlight again. The waves were still high. He spotted the keel of the over-turned boat, and pushed his way toward it, finally making it.

Using all his strength, he pushed the boat toward the shore and struggled to flip it over. It jammed on the rocks, and he pulled the extra oars from their fastenings, using them to overturn it. He was relieved to see it was damaged only along the gunwale and not stove in as he'd feared. He could repair it, and for the moment it would float. He pulled it close to shore, wedging it between two rocks where the water was calmer. Then he stood, dripping and freezing cold, and scanned the river for Taima.

The Indian was nowhere in sight. He waited, his eyes sweeping the broken moonlit water for any sign of the man. Finally, he spotted a strange-shaped rock on the far bank, then realized it was a human form, Taima's still body draped across the rocks. Fargo hopped into the boat and cast off, fighting the river's current as he cut across, landing yards downstream from Taima's unmoving form. He tethered the boat securely, then hiked back up-stream. Taima was lying facedown, spread across two rocks close to shore. Fargo shook his shoulder, and there was no response. He turned him up. Taima's eyes were shut, and his skin was cold. His face had been battered, and one forearm dangled, broken. But he was still breathing.

Fargo hoisted the man over his shoulder and waded ashore and down to where the boat was moored. They were miles and miles away from Barnes and his men now, Fargo realized. And he doubted that they would hazard those rapids by night in order to follow them. As it was, he and Taima had barely got through alive.

There were a few hours of darkness left, and Fargo knew he'd have to risk making a fire to warm Taima up. The man was still unconscious and shivering. And his broken arm needed to be set. In a few minutes a huge pile of dry driftwood was laid down and crackling brightly. He lay Taima down beside it, put fire-warmed stones around him, and covered him with a blanket. Then he changed to dry clothes and put his wet ones around the fire to dry out.

He found a pair of short straight sticks and then tore up one of his old shirts to make bandages. Then he set to work on Taima's forearm. The Indian's eyes blinked open and focused on him as soon as Fargo had grasped the arm to get the bones realigned. Taima seemed to understand what was happening, and his eyes gave silent permission. As Fargo wrenched the arm into a straight position, Taima's breath stopped and his face seemed to turn to stone, but his gaze never wavered and he didn't cry out. It hurt like hell, Fargo knew, as he positioned the sticks on either side of the forearm and bound them into position with the torn strips of fabric.

When it was finished, Fargo rose and went to retrieve some food from the canoe. Taima struggled to sit up, tentatively touched the cuts on his face, then his splinted arm.

"You could be medicine man," Taima said appreciatively. He wiggled his fingers and winced with pain.

"After one moon," Fargo said. "Maybe two, you can use that arm again."

Taima got to his feet slowly, went down to the river, and washed the blood from his forehead and cheeks. He moved like an old man. Clearly, the raging water had battered him and wounded his body in more ways than were outwardly apparent.

As long as they had a fire, they might as well cook up a good meal. There was no telling when they'd have another opportunity. Fargo boiled a pot of hot coffee and fried up a rasher of bacon. He found some flour and made pancakes, which he topped with molasses.

Taima ate with relish and then took a second cup of coffee. The Havasupai's thoughts seemed to be far away as he stared into the fire.

"Never I think be in boat on this river," Taima said. "Me, either," Fargo said. It was too dark to see much beyond the circle of the firelight, Fargo's mind's eye was filled with images of the pagoda-like rocks that towered as much as a mile above them, the cathedral archways of red and yellow stone, the stripes of layered colored rock, tumbled walls, and vast stillness of the stones. And his ears were filled with the constant rushing of the Colorado River, the powerful cutting water that had carved this stupendous canyon over countless centuries.

"That's one helluva strong river to carve out all this rock," Fargo commented distractedly.

"Hackataia did not make canyon," Taima said in a surprised voice.

"What's Hackataia?"

"Hackataia is—roaring—noise," Taima said, pointing to the river. He made a sound like the rushing water.

"You mean the Colorado River."

"It was many many moons ago," Taima said, settling the blanket around his shoulders. Fargo recognized the usual beginning of an Indian tale. "More moons than are stars in the sky, there came a flood. So much water that the People under the Sun are drowning, all People villages wash away, all People horses and dogs wash away. Then comes the giant of the village, man taller than any tree, bigger than any mountain. He sees the water, and he takes his big knife. Sticks it into the earth."

Taima grabbed a nearby stick and demonstrated.

"This knife of the man so tall, it cracks the earth open, splits the rocks open." Taima made a cracking sound. "All the waters run here, down, the Hackataia, the rushing noise, all the waters ran away from the People. Now the Hackataia is kept here. Not flood all the People again."

"Good story," Fargo said. So that's how the Grand Canyon came to be, according to the Havasupai, Fargo thought as he poured them both another cup of coffee. "Your tribe must have many stories about the river and the canyon."

"Yes," Taima said. "Story about river spirit, too.

Daughter of Havasupai fishes one day in river. Out of water comes river spirit carrying her brother who is dead. So daughter of Havasupai and he . . . make happy." Fargo grinned and nodded as Taima made a gesture to indicate the two having sex. "Then brother comes to life again, walks and smiles. Daughter of Havasupai takes river spirit to Havasupai village and good harvests come for many many summers."

Taima's eyelids drooped, and Fargo realized they didn't have more than a few hours to catch some sleep. They rolled themselves into their blankets against the chilly night. Fargo positioned the Colt by his head, and as he lay down, reminded himself to wake well before dawn so that they could be on their way before Barnes and his men caught up with them.

Fargo woke to the sound of a loud ke-woow of the brown-crested flycatcher. He opened his eyes to see the sky growing pale with the coming of dawn on the flat desert high above. The canyon still held the cold dark night. Here, at the bottom of the canyon, the sun wouldn't rise until mid-morning. The fire was glowing with the last embers. After the full meal and a few hours of sleep, Fargo felt refreshed. It was time to move on.

The battering of the river had hurt Taima badly, Fargo saw. The Indian moved even more slowly this morning, though he tried to pretend that everything was all right. Fargo doused the embers with water, then buried the telltale firepit deep in sand until no smoke rose. There was no way to know how far Barnes and his men were behind them now, but one thing was for certain, he did not want to leave any trace of their campfire that might be a clue to their progress. Better to keep Barnes and his men guessing.

It took another half hour to repair the gunwale of the boat, which had been broken in one place by the force of its collision with the rocks. Using the repair tools, Fargo braced it with a piece of driftwood and hammered over patches of the extra sheets of tin. It would hold. The keel was dented and battered, but was all right.

With a final glance around the sandbar to make sure they were leaving no visible trace, Fargo got into the boat with Taima and they cast off. Cold shadows still blanketed the bottom of the canyon, although high above rocks shaped like castle turrets were glowing with the golden light of morning. A half mile down the river, they encountered another rapid with boiling white water, submerged rocks, and plummeting chutes. Fargo found that in the morning light, and with the experience of the last two days, it was easy to negotiate. For the next few hours, they made good time, shooting the exciting white water patches, then floating lazily with the big muddy river between towering cliffs of layered color.

The sun finally rose in mid-morning and drove away the chill in the air. Here the canyon widened, and on either side of the river, he glimpsed layer after layer of high rock spires ascending toward the lip of the canyon, stone striped with dark red, chocolate-brown, cinnamon, rounded like mammoth elephant backs or pointed like the spires of churches. A flock of mountain sheep with their spiraled horns skittered up the slope on spindly legs. Eagles nested in the cliffs and drifted against the sky.

As they floated along, Taima fell asleep. Fargo pulled the box with their pistols near him, then surveyed the clouds, sniffed the air. There was rain due. If not in the canyon, then on the high desert plains around the Grand Canyon. As the hours passed, the sun appeared and disappeared behind the thickening layers of gray and white. For a while in the distance he could see the tall anvil head of a thunderstorm taking shape, but then the lower clouds obscured his view and seemed to close off the top of the canyon, trapping them inside.

Taima awoke at midday and looked around at the landscape. He pointed to a huge outcropping of reddish stone and called to it in his language. Fargo figured they must be getting close to the Havasupai lands. But where the hell were Paulina and Bishy? He hoped they hadn't somehow passed by in the night.

"River gets angry soon," Taima said, looking ahead anxiously. He pointed up ahead. "Only dead men walk on this water."

Deadman Rapids. Fargo had heard a river man once talk about this stretch of the Colorado River, which nobody had ever tried before, but had only seen from far above. It was white water so bad, it was like nowhere else. They had gone another half mile when he heard the sound of it up ahead, the noise of the tons of water as it fell downward, dashing against the rocks, pouring its power over the boulders, whirling and eddying.

Unaccountably, he was seized by the desire to shoot it, to take the boat straight down it rather than to portage, to test himself against the river's might and cunning. But it wouldn't be prudent to rush right in, he told himself. If he was going to best the river, he'd have to be wise. Slow. Just as cunning as its deceitful and powerful waters.

As the water began to quicken, he steered the boat to the center of the river, proceeding from chute to chute as the rocks grew larger, the river began to tilt downward. Ahead, was the roar of falling water. He shot down a smooth unruffled V and stalled the boat in a backwater, handed the oars off to Taima, and rose up a little to scan the river down below.

"We carry the boat?" Taima sounded nervous.

"Only if we have to," Fargo said. His eyes had learned much about the river in the past few days, had come to know its habits, had learned to better read the subtle signs on the water's surface—the slight undulation that meant submerged rocks, the smooth rills that indicate backwater. And then there was the boiling white water that could hide anything beneath it, where the mist rose up above. Below, the whirlpools spun crazily. His eyes traced a path down the river, a possible way. Yes. He tied down the box with their pistols in case they should overturn again.

"Get ready to bail," he shouted above the roar of the water. He took the oars from Taima and moved them out of the eddying backwater and into the current. The swift water hurried them along, and Fargo aimed to one side of a whale-size boulder. The boat dropped through space, its bow plunging into the foaming white water, then bobbing up as the back crest hit them, soaking them with the freezing cold water. Taima bailed madly as they emerged, bobbing upward.

Fargo fought the current with his powerful arms, propelling the boat hard right toward another chute. They plummeted down again, the tin clad boat scraping against the rocks, the water pouring over the canvas-topped boat, but surfacing dripping wet and in one piece.

And then came a series of falls so precipitous that Fargo began to wonder if he'd made the right decision, but there was no turning back now. The boat seemed to fall through space, carried over the drops and lunging into the seething foam of the white water, battered again and again by the rocks. Fargo heaved with the oars or used them to push off from boulders in the nick of time, to keep them in the center of the smooth Vs of water, the sloping channels between the rills. At times he felt the boat was falling out of the sky, barely caught time and again by the roiling water. Other times it seemed the boat would surely founder as the back crest held them below a falls and water poured inside, threatening to swamp them. Another time, they spun about crazily in a vigorous whirlpool, until he could break them free with the powerful strokes of the oars.

An hour of fighting the river had exhausted both

of them until finally, after a last stretch of the worse white water yet, the river suddenly calmed to a gentle ripple, reflecting the lead-gray sky up above. They floated out onto the still water, as a chill wind blew on their water-soaked clothes and skin. Fargo breathed a sigh, and Taima laughed delightedly and bailed out the last of the water.

"No more river in the boat. Now we are dead men who walk on the water!" Taima said, laughing in delight.

"Yeah, we made it," Fargo said. He rested the oars. The relief was short-lived. At a bend, he spotted a piece of shattered boat. A piece of wood with tin nailed was wedged between two rocks. He paddled over and pulled it aboard. Farther on he retrieved a battered crate floating free. Fargo swore. It was bound to be Paulina's boat. She hadn't made it through Deadman Rapids.

His eyes swept the riverbanks, the rocky shores, the water-washed rocks in the stream, for any signs. He saw plenty of them piled on the shore. Bits of boat smashed to smithereens.

"Squaw?" Taima asked.

Fargo nodded silently. Out of the corner of his eye, Fargo spotted movement among some rocks onshore. He stared at the spot, but saw nothing. His instinct told him he had. Swiftly, he paddled hard, aiming for the spot. Then he saw pieces of the boat dragged up on the shore. They were halfway to the spot when a shot exploded, a bullet whizzed overhead. But not close. Not close at all. The retort resounded in a booming echo through the rocky cliffs.

"Get down," he said to Taima, hunching himself.

A second shot fired, the bullet kicking up a fan of water as it plunged into the river ahead of him. But this time he'd seen her. It was Paulina, her blond hair unmistakable as she popped up from behind a rock. She was a lousy shot with that derringer. He waved his hands hoping she might recognize him. She popped up again, but before she'd looked, she'd fired. This time, her aim was luckier and the bullet sped by a few feet off the mark to their left. An instant later she appeared to recognize him, and her mouth dropped open in horror. She cried aloud, jumped out from behind the rock, and hurried down toward the waterline as they drew up.

"Well, that's a nice kind of welcome," Fargo said as they hopped out, and he and Taima dragged the boat up onto the shoal.

"Skye!" Paulina fairly shouted. She wrapped her arms around him in a relieved hug. He took the derringer from her grasp and held it in his hand.

"You ever learn to shoot this thing?"

Paulina shook her head no.

"I just have it to scare people off," she said. "It usually works. I don't shoot unless I think I really have to."

Her golden hair was a frizzy nest. She was wearing fringed buckskin pants and shirt, which were soaking wet. When they dried, he thought, they'd be stiff as a board and about as uncomfortable. But her face, sunburned and with a few new freckles across her nose, was glowing with ardor and excitement. Her brown eyes danced with glee.

"Skye! I can't believe you're here at last! How did you find me?"

"Followed the mess you left behind," Fargo said, nodding toward the bits of broken boat lying nearby.

"I salvaged what I could," she said. "I don't quite know what I'm going to do without a boat." She suddenly shrugged. "But isn't this fun?"

Fargo shook her by the shoulders.

"Look, Paulina. You got Cavell Barnes and a bunch of his men right on your tail." Even as he admonished her, he admired her indomitable spirit.

"Slowpokes," she said defiantly. "Those ill-mannered slobs from the saloon? Well, they haven't caught up to me yet."

"Just before they launched at the river they burned out a ranch, shot three men, and raped a woman." Paulina's face grew grave at his words. She nodded, and her brown eyes were suddenly serious. "They're not just out having an adventure," Fargo added.

Paulina shuddered and gazed across the river, her expression troubled. She focused on Taima.

"Who's he?"

Fargo introduced him and explained that the Havasupai tribe lived a short distance downstream. He told her about Inteus.

"A real Indian tribe!" she said. "Oh, I'd like to see that."

"But where's Bishy?" he asked. Paulina slapped her forehead as if suddenly remembering, then led him to the rocks where she'd been hiding.

Aloisha Bishy lay sprawled there, soaking wet, a purplish bruise on his forehead and a goose-egg rising on his pate. His wispy beard and white hair were bedraggled. But he was breathing, steady but shallow, and his skin was warm to the touch.

"He slipped on a rock just as we were struggling to shore," Paulina said. "And hit his head. I dragged him up here."

Damn lucky, Fargo thought. If the old man had been knocked out midstream, he'd have been swept on by the water and have been battered to death or have drowned, whichever came first.

"He'll be all right," Fargo said, propping the old man up against a rock and then covering him with one of the few blankets that had remained dry in a canvas bag. "And I've got some dry clothes in there, too," Fargo said to Paulina. "Those skins are going to turn hard when they dry out."

"Oh, excellent!" Paulina said with a laugh. "These Wild West clothes are awfully uncomfortable," she admitted. She disappeared with a few of his things and then reappeared a few minutes later, wearing a red plaid shirt that set her face aglow along with a pair of his jeans that she had to roll up at the bottom. She donned her fancy boots. Despite the fact that his clothes didn't her well, she looked great.

"We've got to figure out what to do now. Barnes and his men will be along behind us sooner or later," he thought out loud.

Fargo stared at the high canyon walls, the fantastic shapes of the beetle-browed frowning cliffs, the bluish strata of limestone and whitish clay, the red rocks that rose like columns thousands of feet above them, the gray and threatening sky.

There was no way to climb out of the canyon in this part. The only way to get out was by going straight ahead down the river. But now there were four of them with only one boat. While the sturdy craft could carry four of them, it would be far more dangerous in the rapids and would mean they would have to jettison all their supplies and the canvas cover that kept the boat from swamping and sinking when the water poured in over the gunwales. No, they wouldn't make it far that way, either.

While Paulina hovered over Bishy and Taima watched anxiously upstream, Fargo paced the shore. He felt instinctually that Barnes and his men weren't far behind. They had to do something fast, have some plan. He gazed downstream and saw the quiet river drifting in narrow channels between two high red cliffs with thick green bushes at their feet. Here, the river cut into several streams by tall red boulders and beyond them, it turned abruptly. Finally, the outlines of an idea came to him. It was a long shot, such a long shot. Barnes might be too smart to fall for it. And if one thing went wrong, it wouldn't work.

An hour later, all was ready. They had been hurrying to get everything in place, worrying every minute that Barnes and his men would arrive too soon. First Fargo had ferried them, one by one, downstream. Paulina and Bishy, who had come around, hid in the thick bushes by the huge boulders. They took along the broken wreckage of Paulina's boat.

"All right, let's go," Fargo said. He was carrying two long lengths of looped rope as he got into the boat. Taima took the oars and glanced nervously upstream, as if he expected to see boatloads of men appear.

With sure strokes, the Indian quickly ferried him out through the gently running water to the largest of the boulders that rose twenty feet upward. The boat bumped against it. Fargo looped the ropes around his shoulder, located a crack in the rock, and wedged his fist into it, pulling himself upward with his powerful muscles. He jammed the toes of his boots into the rock, slipped, then found a foothold as he ascended. Taima paddled the boat back toward shore, beached it under the thick bushes, and camouflaged it with extra green boughs.

As Fargo climbed the boulder, the rough rock scraped his hands, tore at the knees of his jeans. Finally, he hauled himself on to its peak, and he realized he'd calculated wrong. The flat top of the rock inclined slightly and even lying down flat, he'd be fully visible from upstream. It wasn't going to work, damn it.

Just then, he spotted movement. A boat, yes, two, then three, small objects bobbing up and down, tumbling down the white water. Barnes and his men, and they were about to descend the worst of Deadman Rapids. And here he was sitting on top of a boulder, visible as a sitting duck.

5

The tiny shapes of the boats bobbed up and down in the distance, way upstream. Fargo looked around in desperation. There was nowhere to hide on the top of the boulder. And with every passing second, Barnes or one of his men might spot him. Suddenly, he threw himself down and peered over the downstream side of the huge boulder. Below the crest of the rock, a few feet below was a crack and a shorter part of the rock that formed a kind of ledge. It was perfect.

Fargo vaulted off the top of the rock, landing, teetering for a moment, off balance high over the rushing water below. Then he regained his footing and hunched down. The higher part of the boulder hid him upstream, and the lip of the lower one shielded him from the view of downstream. But he was poised a dozen feet or more over the narrow channel of smooth water that slipped beside this rock on either side.

The question was, which way would they come? The whole thing was risky, he thought as he slipped the ropes off his shoulder and knotted two lassos. He scanned the channel. Barnes and his men might opt to navigate through the more shallow part of the river that was far out of his reach. In that case his whole plan would fall through. Yeah, it was a risk, but everything was.

He eased himself up to look over the top of the rock, his hands holding the lassos as his eyes searched for the approaching boats. They weren't there. He swore, then spotted them on the far bank above the last of Deadman Rapids. There were the small figures of men unloading supplies from the four boats and carrying them on their shoulders along the rocky shoreline. Hell, Barnes was cannier than he thought. They'd decided to portage rather than risk the worst of the dangerous white water.

Fargo looked over to shore where Taima hid with Paulina and Bishy in the thick bushes. Taima signaled upstream. Fargo nodded to indicate that he'd seen Barnes and the approaching men. Then he rested against the rock for a while. There'd be a wait now. He thought about his plan again. Would it still work? He decided to take the chance. Maybe, just maybe, Barnes would fall for it, even if they hadn't shot the rapids.

An hour later, Barnes and his men had nearly finished transporting and loading up the boats and were assembling on the opposite bank somewhat upstream, about to launch. Above the roar of the water, Fargo could hear their occasional shouts.

From time to time, he eased himself up and took a look at them. Platan Arnez was there, his arm bound up from the bullet he'd taken back in Nowhere. The gray-haired Barnes directed the action from a tall rock. And Fargo spotted the tall figure of Inteus, too. The Havasupai stood gazing downstream in his direction. Fargo ducked and hoped he'd not been spotted. The Indian's instincts were probably as well honed as his own. Inteus might be suspecting that someone was downstream, waiting for them. Maybe he even felt the presence of his brother, Taima, nearby.

Fargo checked the lassos again, looped them loosely, checked that they were tied at one end securely around a sharp tooth of the boulder. He ducked down between the rocks, checking to see which spot would allow him to remain out of sight as the boats passed so near. Then he heard a shout and peered out to see that the first boat was launched and then the second. A glimpse of the gray head of Barnes—and Inteus in the stern, his figure alert and tense. There were four boats. He hunched down and waited, ready.

An instant later he heard voices close by and glimpsed a boat passing just below, then a second. Yes, they were choosing the large smooth channel just below him. He pressed against the rock so he wouldn't be spotted. And waited. Then the third boat came on, slipping between rocks some distance away. He cursed, felt the seconds passing, his muscles tense and tight with the waiting, hoping for a longer delay so that the other three boats would be well out of sight around the bend. The sky was threatening rain, and Fargo heard the rumble of distant thunder.

Where was the fourth boat? Just then, he heard a splash, an oar dipping, a sudden sound against the background roar of the water. Fargo came to his feet, poised and tense as the fourth boat slipped into view. There were two men in it, one short and heavy with a pudgy face and pig eyes. The other was rangy and dark with a swarthy complexion and a greasy-looking leather vest.

The rope lasso snaked out across the air, a fluttering circle that fell heavily around the two men. The two looked up in astonishment and an instant later, the second lasso arced through space, catching both men again around the torsos. The forward motion of the boat pulled the ropes taut, drawing the two men close together, swinging the boat around sideways and threatening to capsize it. The ropes groaned under the strain.

The two men shouted and struggled, trying to get to their guns. But their arms were pinioned to their sides by the cuttingly tight rope, and they were pulled close together. They hunched down desperately against the gunwales as the boat tipped precipitously and threatened to overturn. Then it jammed sideways against a rock and came to a halt.

Fargo looked downstream. He'd been lucky. Barnes and the other boats were out of sight beyond the bend of the river. Nevertheless, he had to move fast now. He grasped the rope that descended in a diagonal line and swung out, hand over hand, down toward the boat. Despite his arms pinned tight against him, the short pig-eyed one managed to get his pistol drawn and pulled it upward as Fargo swayed on the rope, approaching hand over hand. The man brought the barrel up, just as Fargo kicked out. The pistol went flying out of the man's grasp and landed with a splash in the river.

The two men tried to rise, to knock him out of the boat as he swung aboard. He pulled his Colt and reversed it, cold-cocking the pig-eyed man who slumped down, dragging the other downward. As the tall one fell, Fargo saw him fumbling for his gun. Then it was in his hand. The man rolled sideways, his face clouded with fury. He pointed the pistol upward and started to squeeze the trigger. But just then the boat lurched, he rolled forward and the gun went off. The force of the bullet jolted the tall man's body. Then he lay still and didn't move again.

Using his one good arm, Taima had already launched the boat from shore and was nearly there, paddling awkwardly with the oar braced against his shoulder. Loaded in the boat were the bits of Paulina's smashed boat. Taima threw them overboard into the center of the current, bit by bit, and let them drift downstream. When the fourth boat didn't appear and Barnes saw bits of wreckage drifting by, he might assume it had come to grief. On the other hand, this passage was easy, no white water. Would he be suspicious? Suspect a trick? He might order some of his men to retrace their steps upstream and take a look. In that case there was no time to lose.

In a few minutes Fargo had ascended the rock again and untied the ropes, and they had ferried both boats to shore. Paulina got to work cutting green leafy switches from the bushes to hide them completely. The danger wasn't over yet. There was still the possibility that Barnes and his men would come back looking around.

Fargo tied the unconscious pig-eyed man securely. Then he armed Bishy and Paulina with rounded stones and gave them the job of watching over the pig-eyed man and knocking him out again if he came around. Taima hid the dead body of the taller one deeper into the bushes. It had started to rain. Large cold drops fell at first, splattering the rocks, deepening the colors of the stone to darker reds and oranges. Fargo wondered what was happening downstream.

He gazed up the bank behind them and saw a crack in the rock. He climbed up a short distance to investigate and saw that he could climb somewhat hidden by the crease in the rock, upward and to the top of the promontory. From the top, he guessed, he would have a good view.

He began ascending as the rain fell more steadily around him. The dry coarse earth seemed to resist the rain at first, then turn instantly to slippery mud. The rocks were wet and slick. It was hard going, some of the tumbled rock threatening to landslide as he carefully climbed, keeping an eye out below in case any of Barnes' men should come into sight on the river. The muddy water fell away down below him as he climbed higher, and he felt lighter when he could see farther, as if the weight of the imprisoning canyon was left far behind him. All around him lay the complex land, cut and scored, carved deep and ravaged by the water and wind and heat and cold.

The rain was heavier now, obscuring the view of the distant cliffs in layers of wavering gray veils. He reached the top and hauled himself up. He was nowhere near the top of the canyon of course, which rose in a series of rugged towers higher and higher on either side of him. But far below him lay the muddy flow of the Big Colorado River, and from here he could see around the next bend of the river, where it turned back and forth around a series of short cone-shaped hills. The distance disappeared in a gray sheet of falling rain.

Fargo pulled the hat brim low, and the water ran off it in a stream. His eyes searched the clouded view as the rain poured in harder until he could barely see the broken rocks and the sinuous line of the river down below. He thought he spotted something on a bend in the river some distance downstream, but then he lost sight of it again as the rain swept in. The thunder rolled in the clouds above, and lightning cracked, struck the top of a distant butte, then struck again, a jagged line fluttering. The clap of thunder boomed and echoed through the rocks. He looked again at the spot hidden in the rain. He was soaked through to the skin. He took shelter from the downpour by hunching against a rock where there was a slight overhang.

After another ten minutes, the rocks and hills

gradually reappeared. The rain lifted, and the gray clouds, scudding fast above the canyon, came into view again. Fargo stared again at the spot and then saw them. Yes, he'd been right. There were the tiny figures of Barnes and his men with their three remaining boats. He counted eight men. They had obviously lost another boat somewhere upstream and had to travel with two of the boats holding three men.

The tiny figures stood by the shore for a long time, apparently looking upstream. Then one of them waded out into the water and returned to shore. It was too far to see any detail, but Fargo guessed they'd spotted pieces of Paulina's boat floating by and figured it was their own missing boat. They paced on the bank for another fifteen minutes. The sun came out, flooding the wet canyon with the golden light of afternoon, lancing rays that cut through the landscape. The high-piled clouds glittered with edges of burnished bronze. A rainbow arched in the distance, its striped radiance glowing with shifting colors.

Down below, the men got into the three boats and launched. Fargo breathed a sigh of relief, waited to watch them disappear around a distant bend of the river. He'd fooled them. And best yet, Barnes and his men still thought that Paulina and Bishy, as well as the mysterious boat carrying Fargo and Taima that slipped by them in the night, were all downstream of them. So they'd be hunting in the wrong direction. He turned away and descended the rocky and muddy track.

By the time he got back to where the others were waiting, he decided they'd camp for the night. It was only a couple of hours before sunset, and all of them could use a good night's rest. He scouted around the site and found, a short way upstream, a couple of shallow caves a good ten feet above the river with a flat ledge in front, perfect for a campfire.

For the next couple of hours, they were busy. They didn't even pause to dry out, but set immediately to work. First they hauled dry driftwood up to the ledge along with the supplies from both boats. The short pig-eyed man came back to consciousness but refused to talk. He was startled when he caught sight of Taima, probably mistaking him for Inteus. But then he apparently had figured out they weren't the same man, especially since Taima had his arm in a splint. Fargo got him to his feet and tied him securely to a rock at the entrance to one of the caves, then returned to the riverbank to find Taima eyeing the river.

"River spirit is angry," Taima said.

The river was running muddy now and rising fast. Fargo knew how dangerous flash floods could be. The river was carrying off all the water that had fallen in the vicinity. But how much rain had fallen in all the side canyons and farther upstream? The rain would run off the rocks and dry soil to become a raging torrent.

"Are we camped high enough?" Fargo asked, nodding toward the caves.

"Very angry river," Taima said with a shrug.

Fargo measured the rise of the river and then looked back at the ledge with the caves, where they were planning to rest for the night. He doubted the water would get that high, but still, you could never be sure.

The two of them carried the boats as high as they could and tethered them securely to large boulders. Afterward, Fargo hoisted the corpse of the tall swarthy man up a short slope, and Bishy and Paulina built a rock cairn over him to keep the vultures off.

"It was more than the bastard deserved" was Bishy's grim epitaph before they returned to the rock ledge.

It was nearly sunset. Overhead, the remaining clouds had turned rose-red and fiery-peach. Blue shadows slid across the water and began to fill the canyon. Fargo lit the campfire and changed into fresh dry clothes. Everyone spread their sodden garments around the campfire on rocks to dry out.

Taima selected a spot in the ground, and using a piece of curved tree bark as a shovel, with his good arm began to dig a hole, which he lined with small stones.

"What's he doing?"

"Just watch," Fargo answered Paulina. Taima placed driftwood inside the rock-lined pit, lit a fire, and then returned to the riverbank.

Paulina rested back against a rock and pulled a canvas envelope from inside her shirt. She removed the small leather notebook he'd seen her writing in before, along with her pen and ink bottle. With a small penknife, she sliced open fresh pages of the notebook and began to write. Occasionally, she would stare into the campfire deep in thought. And then she would write a few more sentences.

Fargo lay back against a fire-warmed rock as the light began to fade to the purple dusk. Bishy was dozing. The bump on the head had tired him out. The pig-eyed man tied to the rock caught Fargo's eye occasionally and scowled.

"How about telling me what the hell Barnes is up to, bringing you men down this canyon?" Fargo asked him. "Besides robbing that rancher I mean. What's all this about finding gold?"

The pig-eyed man growled and refused to talk.

"You'll talk soon enough," Fargo said to him, and turned his attention back to admiring Paulina. She looked wonderful in his faded cambray shirt and his jeans, even though they didn't fit her right. She loosed her braid, and her hair spilled down over her shoulders in a shower of golden glinting light.

Taima returned from the riverbank with a string of fresh-caught and cleaned whitefish, a handful of fresh herbs and grasses, and a bundle of mesquite branches. Taima shook his head no when Paulina rose and brought out the fry pan. Instead, Taima laid the mesquite branches into the pit, where the little fire had burned down to embers, then fresh grasses and herbs over the sticks, then layers of the fish and more herbs, until the pit was filled. He covered it with more leaves and some of the hot stones from around the campfire.

Fargo felt the tiredness settle over him as they lounged around the fire and the smells of the Havasupai cooking began to waft out of the pit. The first stars appeared between the clouds. The short man was dozing, his head jerked downward. Fargo rose and piled more wood on the campfire. The red embers danced. He caught Taima's eye and then glanced toward the sleeping man. Fargo picked up a stick with a glowing ember at the tip and handed it to Taima. The Havasupai smiled and nodded, his brown eyes mischievous. Bishy came awake, and Paulina watched the two of them curiously.

Fargo stood above the sleeping man, then kicked his knee with his boot. The pain brought the man awake in an instant. His eyes, small in his bloated face, glanced up to see Fargo standing above him. Taima stood nearby with the flaming brand.

"So. I ask you again. What's Cavell Barnes up to?"

Fargo sat down on a rock near the short man and stared down at him. The man shook his head and compressed his lips tight. The man was scared. It wouldn't take much to break him.

"What about the gold?"

He shook his head again.

"Doesn't want to tell us," Fargo said laconically. "So what's your name, then?"

"Name's Potter." But he refused to say more. Fargo glanced at Taima, who stood slowly with the brand and walked step by step forward, his dark eyes unreadable.

"Yeah, he's a Havasupai," Fargo said as Potter's eyes shifted nervously. "You ever had any dealings with them? No mercy," he lied.

"No," Paulina said as she saw what it looked like they were intending to do. "You can't . . . you can't—"

Fargo silenced her with a look.

"I saw a man one time got tortured by the Havasupai," Fargo continued.

Taima stopped and blew on the tip of the ember until it glowed red, then stuck it in the fire again.

"This man looked like he'd been charred in a campfire," Fargo said. Paulina cried out in fright and got to her feet. "He was black all over. Hardly one inch of skin wasn't burned. Only he was still alive. Those Indians got that figured out, see. How to keep you from dying too fast."

Taima had the tip of the ember glowing now. Potter's pig eyes were wide and scared. Paulina was wringing her hands. Taima took a step forward, his face impassive, staring at Potter.

Paulina rushed forward but Fargo was too quick. He caught her arms and held her back.

"You can't let him do that, Skye," she sobbed. "You can't!"

"Now, hold on here Fargo," Bishy spoke up. "This fellow may be a criminal, but I mean—You can't let this happen." The old man got to his feet nervously, not certain what to do.

"Please, stop, Taima. Please. Skye, stop him!" Paulina said, struggling in his grasp.

"I don't think I can," Fargo lied again. "The

Havasupai are masters at torture. And the fire torture is one of their favorites. They're one of the bloodthirstiest tribes in the West." He smiled to himself at how opposite to the truth that statement was. The Havasupai were one of the most peaceable people he'd ever met and only fought in defense for their own, their village, and their families.

The ember wavered toward Potter, whose mouth gaped like a fish. Taima kept his face completely still, his dark eyes blank. Yeah, he was good at playing the role. Potter was trembling.

"It's . . . it's your tribe got the gold!" Potter sputtered. The glowing brand wavered in front of his eyes. "That's what we's after!"

"What are you talking about?" Fargo shot at him.

"Why, all that gold that them Have-Soups got in caves in their village."

Taima stood stock-still, waving the brand in front of Potter's face.

"Why we done run into one of them Have-Soups. Looks just like this one." Potter nodded at Taima. "Only different. Name's Intaste or something like that."

The words were coming in a rush now. Taima backed up a step and put the brand back in the fire, his eyes never leaving Potter's eyes. Paulina relaxed in Fargo's grip, and he put his arms around her. She was quaking.

"Yeah, this Intaste fellow done told Barnes about this gold those Have-Soups got. How they done stole this gold from the stagecoaches for years and years, and they been hiding it in their village."

Fargo and Taima exchanged glances, and Fargo could tell by the Indian's expression that this information came as a surprise. Obviously, Inteus had been telling lies. But why?

"Those Have-Soups knocking over all those stagecoaches. Goddamn redskins."

Taima made a motion toward the brand, and Potter struggled as if he would cover up his face if his arms weren't tied.

"Present comp'ny except," Potter said toward Taima. He stared around and caught Fargo's eye. "You're the one they call the Trailsman. Barnes got real pissed after he ran into you at that saloon. Said he'd always hated hearing those stories about you. Said he was going to track you down if it was the last thing he did. Said he was going to skin you alive. He'll do it, too. I'd hate to be in your shoes, Trailsman."

"I'd hate to be in yours," Fargo said. He continued to hold onto Paulina. She was trembling against him.

"What the hell're you doing here in the Grand Canyon anyway?" Potter sputtered. "That was you slipped by us the other night in that boat, weren't it? You looking for this dame?"

"*I'm* asking the questions," Fargo said, nodding to Taima. The Indian took the brand out of the fire again.

"Sure, sure," Potter said hastily. "Whad'ya wanna know?"

"What was Barnes planning to do when he reached the Havasupai village?"

"Well, that Intaste guy done told us all about this secret entrance those redskins got. Something about a waterfall."

The brand trembled in Taima's hand, but Fargo knew he was probably the only one who noticed. So his suspicions had been correct. There *was* a secret passage by the waterfall that led from the Grand Canyon up to the Havasupai village in the side canyon high above. Undoubtedly, each member of the tribe was sworn to secrecy. But now Inteus had broken the sacred oath.

"So what about this secret entrance?"

"Well, Intaste was goin' to lead us up there, and we was going to take that village by surprise. Him and Barnes got a deal. If we kilt every last one of them Indians, women and children, too, then old Intaste would show us where the gold was."

"Kill . . . all of them?" Paulina asked, disbelieving.

"Don't ask me why," Potter said. "It's Intaste's own people, and I guess he got his own reason."

Fargo and Taima exchanged silent glances, and Fargo saw the deep hatred that lay in Taima's dark eyes. He knew they were both thinking the same thing. Sure, Inteus had his reasons. He'd been exiled from the tribe. And he wanted revenge. He was using Barnes and his men to slaughter his own tribe, his entire people, by making up this ridiculous story of hidden gold.

"That's horrible," Paulina said. "But if the Indians have been stealing gold all those years, well, that's not right, either." She subsided into silence.

"Only thing Intaste doesn't know," Potter added, "is that Barnes told the rest of us, soon's we find that gold, we gonna kill that redskin, too. Barnes ain't fond of redskins, and me, neither." Potter remembered Taima again and added, "Present comp'ny except."

"I get the picture," Fargo said.

"Only, don't tell Barnes I done gone and tole you all his plans," Potter said nervously.

"Sure," Fargo said distractedly.

"Yeah, this been a good trip for us boys," Potter said. "We done got us a bunch of cash off some sucker rancher. Some of us got a nice piece of ass, too. Yeah, we been doing—"

Fargo threw Paulina to one side and hauled Potter to his feet. The short man's eyes were terrified. Despite the fact that the man's hands were bound, Fargo socked him in the belly, once, twice, and felt the satisfying crunch of breaking ribs and the rush of air leave the man's body. Potter's knees gave way, and Fargo delivered a hard uppercut, snapping his head back. Potter's eyes rolled back in his head, and Fargo tossed him to the ground. Paulina watched him, her eyes wide with fright.

"Yeah, that was for Dofield and his wife," Fargo said silently to himself as he stood over the crumpled form. It was far less than the bastard deserved, but it was a start.

Taima threw down the brand and walked away from the fire and stood looking out at the dark river. Fargo joined him. The rushing sound was louder, the river rising higher as the rain runoff from the desert above streamed into the canyon. The sky was overcast again, no stars in the sky.

"I must go now," Taima said. "I will take the boat and go to warn my people. I must go now."

"No. The river's high," Fargo said. "And you've got only one good arm. There'll be no moon tonight. Without light, you'd never make it. Wait until morning. We'll all go together. We'll have a better chance."

"I must go now," Taima said again. "Village is one day away now. I must go. Now."

From his tone of voice, Fargo knew there was no dissuading him. Taima's loyalty was to his tribe. The possibility that Inteus was leading Barnes and his gang of ruffians ever nearer to the secret entrance to the Havasupai village was making Taima crazy. He paced up and down on the rock ledge.

"I understand," Fargo said. "Tell me how to find your village. I will bring the others tomorrow." It meant four of them together in the boat, and it would mean jettisoning most of their supplies. But with the river running higher than usual, the rocks would be submerged and they would probably be all right. Fargo got Taima to describe the canyon where the waterfall fell directly beneath the Havasupai village. He was careful not to ask Taima how to find the secret entrance. Even though Taima completely trusted him, Fargo knew how sacred such oaths were and he would not ask Taima to betray the secret. He would trust that by the time they arrived there, Taima would be waiting or would send someone to guide them. That is, if Taima could get there before Barnes and Inteus did.

Fargo walked Taima down to the shore. The river was two feet higher, and the bushes where they had hidden were like a waving mass of leafy reeds. The Indian selected the boat that Potter had been in, which was slightly less sturdy. They grasped hands in farewell, and Fargo helped push him off into the roiling water.

"Good-bye, friend," Taima said as he paddled away into the rushing darkness.

After he had gone, Fargo returned to the camp. Paulina sat nervously balanced on a rock, and Bishy was pacing back and forth by the fire. Potter lay crumpled and still. Fargo realized they had not eaten the fish that Taima had buried several hours before. He removed the stones, then the leaves and herbs, as fragrant steam rose up. He lifted the flaky fish onto tin plates and passed some to Paulina and to Bishy. It was delicious, but nobody had much of an appetite. There was a deep silence among them, and Paulina wouldn't catch his eye.

"Eat," Fargo said as Paulina put down the plate she had barely tasted. "You're going to need your strength tomorrow."

Paulina stood and started to move away. Fargo rose, grabbed her arm, and turned her about. Her brown eyes were hard.

"Let me go," she said, wriggling in his grasp. Bishy got to his feet.

"What's the matter now?" Fargo asked her.

"I can't believe you'd let that savage torture that

man," Paulina spat at him. "Even if he is a crook." She glanced at the unconscious form of Potter.

Fargo laughed and let go of her.

"Oh, that," he said. He sat down again and picked up his plate. Suddenly, the food tasted better to him.

"Yes, that!" Paulina said.

"Taima was never going to brand him," Fargo said. Her eyes widened as she took in this information.

"But . . . but you said the Havasupai were torturers—"

"Sure I did," Fargo said. "I'd have said almost anything to get the information out of that bastard. Taima and I were putting on a little act. And it worked."

Paulina sat down abruptly on the rock.

"Sure looked like the real thing to me, too," Bishy said with a chuckle as he sat down. "Sorry I misjudged you, Fargo."

"But . . . what about all that gold? The stagecoaches those Indians have robbed."

"That's the stupidest story I ever heard," Fargo said. "Like most tribes, the Havasupai think white men are crazy, loco, for chasing after gold all the time. They think gold is useless, and they're right. They're no more interested in robbing stagecoaches than they are in wearing hoopskirts. They just want to be left alone."

Fargo told Paulina and Bishy about Inteus, about how he'd been exiled from the tribe and sworn revenge.

"So Taima's gone with the other boat to try to get there first. He's going to try to get a warning to his tribe."

"I see," Paulina said. There were tears in her eyes. "Oh, I got it all wrong. I'm sorry, Skye."

"That's all right," he said.

Paulina came over then and leaned down to kiss him. He reached up, and his fingers tangled in the long waves of her blond hair. Despite the days on the trail, she still smelled faintly of spring violets and tasted sweet. Bishy cleared his throat and got up off his rock.

"I think I'll just take my blanket and sleep over here," the old man said, speaking a little too loudly. "In this far cave over here." He left with a few blankets.

"Finish your dinner," Fargo told Paulina as he added a few more stout logs to the fire and banked it for the night.

Potter groaned and sat up. The short man's eyes were darting around. He was shooting furious looks at Fargo, who ignored him. Paulina felt sorry for him and fed him some of the fish and then gave him a drink of water. Potter shifted around, apparently trying to get comfortable against the rock. He lay down and rolled over once, getting nearer to the fire.

"Oh, no, you don't," Fargo said. He grabbed Potter and dragged him back to the rock, then tied him again to it so he couldn't roll around, bound his ankles, and made sure his hands were tightly bound so he couldn't wiggle them loose during the night.

Paulina put her notebook back into the canvas envelope, began hunting for something on the ground, but then seemed to give up looking for it. Fargo yawned and pulled a pile of blankets from the heap of supplies. He threw one over Potter and took Paulina's arm. Bishy's loud snore came from one of the caves. They headed for the other one.

The shallow cave had a sandy floor and was dry but not particularly warm. Fargo spread several layers of blankets down, then began getting undressed. Paulina was almost as shy as before, but not quite. She pulled a blanket around her as she took off her clothes, but whether from modesty or from the chill in the air, he couldn't tell.

She slipped in beside him, her fragrant sleekness and warmth pressed against him beneath the scratchy wool of the blankets. She shivered as he held her, stroked her arm, then down along her satiny side.

"Skye . . . I'm sorry . . . I—"

"Don't mention it."

"No, I just want to tell you how much I appreciate, well, you coming after me. Really."

He turned her face toward his and kissed her deeply, enjoying the familiar taste of her again, the warm comfort of her full breasts and hard nipples, the tickle of the long waves of her hair, the fragrant musk of her wetness, the warm sheath that opened to him, the comforting feeling of belonging there, inside of her, connected to her as she clung to him. They moved together like gentle waves lapping the shore, slowly, inevitably, and he could feel her tense.

He slowed, kissing her, holding her beneath him in the warmth of the nest of blankets, bringing her again to the brink and then letting them both plunge over, like the moment in the rapids when the boat dropped and he felt the shooting churning spray of the white water, the power of the force of the inevitable coming as he pumped into her. Then they were floating again on the calm waters, lapped by waves, and she was nestled in his arms. The red glow of the embers played against the edge of the cave, and the rush of the river became a lullaby of sleep.

Something woke him. He lay in the near dark and listened. He heard nothing but the roar of the river outside the cave. Bishy's snore. The quiet breathing of Paulina beside him. The faint fall of the coals shifting in the dying fire. But something had awakened him. Fargo rose and swiftly dressed. Colt in hand, he stole out of the cave. The faint light of dawn was already in the sky. Potter was gone.

6

Potter had escaped, the wily bastard.

Where he'd been tied to the rock, the ropes lay like coiled rattlesnakes. Fargo crossed to the spot and examined them. Cut clean through. Hell, where'd he get the knife? Then Fargo remembered the little penknife that Paulina had been using to slice the pages of her notebook. And she'd been looking for something right before they'd turned in for the night. She'd probably dropped it, and Potter had rolled over to retrieve it, then managed to use the tiny blade to saw through his ropes during the long night.

He straightened at the faint sound of a splash, and he ran down to the riverbank just in time to see the dark form of the boat and Potter disappearing downstream between two huge boulders. He scarcely recognized the riverbank, the water had risen a good five feet. The river ran muddy and swift but, except for the huge boulders large as houses, there were hardly any rocks visible in the wide current that carried tangles of branches and driftwood swiftly downstream.

Fargo swore. They'd lost their boat now, and worse, Potter would soon catch up to Barnes and tell him everything. So Barnes would know they were upstream of him and that Taima was trying to get past them to warn his tribe. Hell.

Just then, Fargo saw a dark form floating in the water. A huge log with several branch stubs was floating by. He dove into the rushing water, swimming with powerful strokes until he reached it, then he hoisted himself up. Just then the log spun about and banged against one of the huge boulders, smashing his leg. Stars danced in front of his eyes as he pushed against the rock with his arms, turning the log about to guide it into the current. It moved slowly, then began floating through.

This was a helluva bad idea, Fargo thought to himself as he lay on the log and struggled to stay on top. By holding on to the nubs of two broken branches and shifting his weight from side to side, he could barely manage it. Every moment, the log threatened to roll over. He was soaking wet. The river was running fast. He pulled himself up and gazed ahead, then spotted the shape of the boat and Potter a few hundred yards ahead. He thought of his pistol, but the Colt in his holster was surely waterlogged and wouldn't fire.

He glanced behind him but could no longer see the spot where Paulina and Bishy were. When he caught up with Potter, he'd hike back and rescue them. Better that than that Potter alerted Barnes where they were and all the men lay in wait for them downstream.

Fargo tried to paddle using his hands. The goddamn log was hard to steer and impossible to hurry. They went around another bend in the river. The light grew stronger in the clear sky above. Dawn, up on the desert plateau, was breaking. Potter hadn't bothered to even turn around and look behind him, thinking that without a boat it would be impossible for Fargo to pursue him.

He continued to paddle the log, using his powerful arms to gather speed as they went down the river. He was gaining on Potter. As he came nearer, he began to paddle underwater only, so the sound of splashing wouldn't attract his attention. Potter seemed to be resting his oars. Then Fargo heard the sound of rapids ahead. Potter obviously heard it too because he suddenly half rose in the boat and peered anxiously ahead.

With a few last desperate strokes, Fargo caught up to Potter, and the log bumped into the boat. Potter waved his arms wildly in the air as he tottered unbalanced. Fargo grabbed the gunwales and struggled to get himself aboard. Potter regained his footing and turned to see Fargo there. He shouted something and kicked one foot.

Fargo ducked and reached up just in time to grab the booted foot before it smashed into his face. He pulled hard, and Potter fell heavily in the boat. Something was in his hand. Paulina's penknife. Half in the boat, Fargo kept hold of Potter's foot and used it to pull himself aboard.

Potter rolled toward him and lashed out. They fought with a silence that was deadly. Fargo felt a burning pain across his shoulder and knew the penknife had slashed deeply. The boat rocked back and forth with their movements, water sloshing over the sides. The roaring of the waters increased. Potter might look like a stocky little man but he was a helluva fighter, Fargo found.

They grappled for the knife, Potter's arm trembling in Fargo's powerful grip. He dropped the knife in the bottom of the boat just as Fargo was about to seize it, then feinted right. Fargo lashed out and connected with Potter's chin. The boat lurched as the small man hit the deck, crawled on all fours, and shook his head dazedly. Fargo glanced downstream and saw the rapids dead ahead, bad ones showing white even with all the floodwaters.

Suddenly, Potter was on him again having found the penknife. It bit him again, a savage slash, in the meat of his shoulder, then across the cheek. He tasted the hot silvery taste of his own blood.

The boat smashed against a rock, throwing both of them nearly out. Fargo regained his footing and threw himself on Potter, determined to best him now. He grabbed the hand with the knife and beat it again and again on the side of the boat until the knife fell out. Potter spit in his face and tried to knee him in the groin. Fargo gave him a powerful left in the jaw, and Potter's head rolled. The boat was lurching through the rapids now, plunging over the precipices. Water suddenly poured in from all sides. Without the canvas covers the empty boat would founder. There was nothing to bail out with, and the oars had gone overboard.

The boat plummeted down another chute, half sunk. Potter was almost unconscious but managed to hang on as the boat wildly spun out of control over the white-crested foam. Suddenly, Fargo heard another sound above the roar of the water. He peered ahead at the river where it calmed below the rapids and saw the shapes of boats ahead in the reflected light of dawn. He counted four and wondered if he was seeing straight. There was no time to wonder how they'd got their hands on another boat. A shot rang out, but it was too far for a true aim. At least from a lurching boat. Yeah, he'd been spotted.

Without oars there was no damn way to stop the swamped boat from tumbling downstream, and the line of four boats downstream could see that. They signaled to one another and then spread out in a line across the current to intercept him. One man in each boat was keeping it steady, stalled in the current, while the other men rose to their knees, rifles at the ready.

Fargo tried desperately to push the boat off the rocks then and maneuver it to the shore. But the current was carrying him too fast. While he was trying to do this, Potter roused himself and spotted the other men. He shouted and waved. Their boat began to spin out of control like a top, the sides of the canyon whirling around them. Fargo realized that in another moment, he would be swept right up to the four boats and they'd have a clear shot at him. This time they'd be too close to miss him.

There was no choice. As he stood up suddenly, a hail of bullets whizzed through the air. He felt the hot fire of a slug slice his side and then he was overboard, diving into the cold dark water. He dove deep, scraped against the rocky bottom, felt the current carry him like dark hands, pushing onward. If it were not for the flood, he would have been battered to death, he knew, but the extra depth of the water carried him over most of the rocks.

Bullets fell around him harmlessly, slowed by the water. He held his breath, and his lungs began to burn, his throat constricted. He let his mind go dark and the water carry him on and on, bashing him against rocks, then hurrying him on. Then he felt himself rising up, up, his head spinning. He broke through to light, took a breath that scorched his lips and throat, not stopping to look around, then dove down again, determined to stay down below in the arms of the river. Again and again, he rose to breathe, then dove, the current bouncing him over the rocks again.

Then he came up for a breath again, dashed the water out of his eyes, and saw, against the whirling sky of light, the shape of boats farther upstream. A tangle of branches drifted swiftly by, and he stroked toward it, reached out to grasp it, ducked beneath the water, and came up inside the cage of branches, hidden from their eyes.

He inhaled again and again until the burning in

his lungs stopped and his head cleared. The four boats were fanned out across the river, the men standing with their rifles at the ready, peering anxiously into the raging waters trying to find him, firing into the muddy stream occasionally. The thicket of branches floated swiftly downstream, and he tucked his legs up under him so that he wouldn't get caught on the bottom. After another moment Barnes signaled, and the four boats headed to shore. They had given up trying to find him.

When he had gone around a bend and they were lost from sight, Fargo spotted a huge floating branch, a thick one the shape of a Y. He pulled himself onto it and lay across the fork. The wood submerged under him but held him above the waves, and it was steady. The cuts on his shoulders and the track of the bullet along his ribs burned like hell. But at least the icy water had stopped the bleeding.

The sky was light above him, whirling again. The branch held him barely above the waves. From a distance he seemed to hear the roar of rapids again and then realized the branch had come to a halt and was wedged between two rocks. He had lost consciousness. He raised his head and looked around.

Above him, on the far north side of the mighty Colorado River, rose a mammoth column of ocher rock. The branch had come to rest at the mouth of a clear smooth stream that met up with the big muddy river. The deep stream ran between tumbled cliffs with a series of shelves covered by tufted green grass.

He recognized the place by Taima's description. This was the mouth of Havasu Creek, he realized. And if he followed the stream, he would come to the waterfall and the secret entrance to the Havasupai village that lay in the side canyon hundreds of feet above the Colorado River. He dragged himself to his feet, feeling the effects of the battering from the river. Suddenly, a dark round shape caught his attention. Something floating out in the stream. He waded out into the muddy water and caught it. A body. He knew whose it was.

He pulled the still cold form toward the mouth of Havasu Creek, then up onshore and turned him over. Taima's dark eyes stared up unseeing into the morning sky. His throat had been slit with one long gash, almost ear to ear, but the water had washed away the blood and his skin looked unreal, like a ghost made of clay, his dark hair plastered on his forehead, the lips almost blue and open as if about to speak one last word.

Fargo knew exactly what had happened. Hadn't Taima said that his brother Inteus never slept and could see in the dark?

Obviously, Inteus had spotted Taima's boat as he tried to slip by Barnes and his men in the night. And this time there had been no mistake. Fargo knew that the Indian's throat had been slit by the hand of his brother. That explained how Barnes got his hand on the extra boat.

It was uncanny he had spotted Taima's corpse

just at the moment it floated by the creek. It was as if Taima's spirit had been trying to get to the village to warn his people of the coming invasion. He couldn't leave the body of Taima here. Nor did he have time to bury it. No, it ought to be returned to his people. It would be hard going up Havasu Creek, Fargo thought. He hoped it wasn't far. He looked about for some driftwood to fashion a travois, but then realized he had no rope to tie the body on.

He knelt and hoisted the corpse over his shoulders, then set off, wading upstream, staying close to the water's edge. It was a long, exhausting morning. He kept going mile after mile, at times walking beside the water on a narrow strip of rocky earth, other times wading in the gently flowing water, which sometimes reached his waist. Along about midday, he heard the sound of rushing water and knew he was approaching the falls.

He rounded a bend in the canyon and saw the falling water ahead of him, an extraordinary white ribbon, a couple hundred feet tall, tumbling almost unbroken down the rocky hill. It was a beautiful spot. All around, the hillsides were covered with plants of all kinds, from the barrel cactus to prickly pears to the radiating spines of the ocotillo and the white-flowered feather-dusters. Fargo stared at the waterfall and the hills, wondering where the secret entrance to the Havasupai village could be. The canyon looked to be impassable, the sheer rock walls on either side of the waterfall too steep for even the spry mountain goats. Just then he caught a movement among the rocks.

A moment later a woman appeared, her face beaming with smiles. She chattered in the Havasupai tongue as she hurried toward him. He couldn't catch anything she said.

She was beautiful but strange, her round eyes lit by an inner radiance. Her face was painted with a red circle high on each cheek and what appeared to be a tattooed line of dots on her chin. Through her pierced ears were loops of bright blue beads, which hung also around her neck and reflected the sun. Her long hair was caught back from her face and braided neatly down her back, and her figure was lithe. Although she was very short, she was willowy, dressed in a simple doeskin dress. He guessed her age about sixteen.

She was talking excitedly, completely ignoring Taima's body, dancing around him. She was talking too fast for him to catch anything. Then she fell to her knees on the soil and began making signs in the earth. It looked like some kind of religious ceremony.

"I don't understand," Fargo said. He pointed at his chest and said his name.

"Fargo," she repeated several times with a laugh. She touched her forehead and said, "Onawa. Onawa."

He repeated her name, and she clapped her hands. Then he pointed at Taima and said his name.

"Taima," the girl repeated, then drew more signs into the earth.

"Bad," Fargo said, using the few words he remembered in their tongue. He pointed down the creek behind him to indicate the coming trouble. "Inteus. Bad."

Onawa laughed then, clapped her hands, and got to her feet.

"Inteus. Bad!" she agreed, laughing and chattering, fairly jumping around. She pulled at his hand to get him to follow her.

If only she spoke English. Confused, he followed. If he could just get her to take him up the secret path to the village above, he could find somebody there who would understand, make them understand that Inteus was on his way with a bunch of desperate men with guns who intended to kill them all.

He hoisted Taima's body over his shoulder again and followed. She led him along a faint trail farther into the canyon. They passed the falls and came to a rocky cliff, where she stopped. Fargo saw a blanket open on the ground. Lying on it were two dozen white trumpet flowers of jimson weed. Poison. Deadly poison. If you picked a jimson flower and then licked your hand, it could make you sick. A little of the plant's milky juice could paralyze you. Enough of it would kill. Obviously, she'd been harvesting them. Did she know what she was doing?

She stopped and looked expectantly at him. He

laid Taima's body down again. Then she pulled at his hands again.

"Bad," he said pointing at the flowers.

Onawa giggled and showed him two sticks, then demonstrated how she plucked the flowers and did not touch them, dropping them carefully. She looked back at him expectantly as he watched her at her task. Onawa was flirting with him, without a doubt.

Again, she pulled on his hand as if to communicate something, but he couldn't figure out what. Finally, Onawa took hold of her dress and suddenly pulled it off over her head and threw it down on a patch of yellow bunch grass. She stood before him, stark naked, her tawny skin gleaming in the light. Her breasts were young and firm, small with dark tipped nipples and large maroon aureole. Her narrow waist curved inward and below her concave belly was the patch of dark fur, her narrow thighs taut and muscular. He let his eyes run over her, and despite his confusion, felt his manhood harden, strain against his jeans.

What the hell was going on? Onawa stepped toward him and pulled at his hand, placing it on her breast. He felt her warmth, the soft roundness of her. She brushed up against his hard cock, felt it beneath the fabric of his clothing, touched it hesitantly, then came into his arms, hungry, wanting, already excited for him.

He lowered her to the ground, unfastened his jeans. He stood out straight and ready for her as she opened her legs to him and he drove inside her, as if entering a dark cave in the earth, its hot wetness tight around him, driving into her strangeness as she took his hands to cover her small breasts. He squeezed the nipples, and Onawa writhed beneath him, her hips pumping upward to meet him, arcing under him in abandon and he felt the coming into her, the gathering of force, the sudden fast and hot stream that exploded up into her heat as he drove harder, deeper, and her legs opened to take his long pumping rod deeper.

She cried out, bucking beneath him, murmuring words he could not understand, squeezing him, and he came, shatteringly, fully, in a fountain of release, all heat and whirling until he was spent and he fell across her.

A moment later he rolled to one side and gazed at her. She smiled at him and began chattering again, her dark eyes dancing. For the life of him, he couldn't figure out what she was up to. Havasupai women, from what he'd heard, were usually pretty standoffish. This one had attacked him like a cougar in heat. But there was no more time to wonder. Every second that passed brought Inteus and the attackers closer and closer to the Havasupai village. He had to make her understand that danger was on the way and that she had to take him to the village elders.

"Inteus. Bad," he said as he pulled on his clothes. He pointed down the creek. He repeated the words and made a slicing motion across his neck, then pointed at Taima's body.

"Taima. Brother," Onawa said nodding and

pointing to herself. He wasn't sure he understood her correctly.

"Inteus. Brother? Too?" he asked.

Onawa nodded again vigorously. But she sure didn't look upset that Taima was dead. She rose, donned her dress, then picked up Taima's hand, patted it, and looked expectantly at his face as if waiting for him to come to life.

Then Fargo realized what had happened. He remembered the story that Taima had told him. About the Havasupai maiden who met the river spirit walking out of the water carrying the body of her brother. After the spirit and the maiden made love, the brother came back to life and the tribe had good harvests forever. Hell, the girl thought he was some kind of river god.

He realized he'd have to use it to get to the village. He stood and pointed up to the waterfall.

"Go," he said. "Village."

Onawa understood that and gathered up the jimson flowers by tying the corners of the blanket together, careful not to touch the deadly flowers. She slung the blanket over her shoulder.

"What?" he asked, pointing to the blanket and the flowers inside. She didn't understand the question, and her dark eyes were puzzled. Fargo cupped his hands like the jimson trumpet flowers and asked again.

She understood now and spoke again in a stream of Havasupai tongue. But seeing his incomprehension, she stopped, then mimed a bow and arrow, being shot with an arrow and falling to the ground.

Fargo understood immediately. She had been gathering the jimson flowers to make the poison that the Havasupai used on the tips of their arrows. Of all the tribes in the West, Fargo had heard that only the mysterious Indians living in the Grand Canyon used poison arrows.

He hoisted Taima over his shoulders again and followed as Onawa led off. The trail was steep and hidden behind rocks. The entrance was a crack between two boulders that seemed so narrow, he wasn't sure at first he could fit through. He had to slip through himself first, then pull Taima's body through after him. He never would have found the entrance on his own, he realized. He'd been lucky that the girl had been there. He shook his head in wonderment. What would Onawa do when she found out he wasn't the river god? He felt badly that then she would have to face the fact her brother was dead forever.

On the other side of the rocky entrance, the path ascended a rocky culvert. At times he had to climb with one hand grappling for handholds, meanwhile steadying Taima's body to keep it from slipping off his shoulders. It was a helluva climb. Taima wasn't exactly light, and he was bone-weary from the dip in the river. Every step up the trail took a concentrated effort. Meanwhile, the ravine rose up around as they continued climbing higher and higher.

After an hour, they were walking along a steep path that clung to the side of a cliff. Far below he could see the top of the waterfall and Havasu

Creek as it ran between the ruddy cliffs down toward the Big Colorado. Onawa suddenly called out and ran ahead of him, disappearing around a corner. He struggled to follow her, nearly lost his balance, then came around the bend. Before him, the trail opened out to a large rocky shelf. Several Havasupai braves stood looking expectantly toward him. The zing of arrows greeted him.

Onawa screamed, cried out. He felt the sting of an arrow as it buried itself into his shoulder. Fargo threw himself forward, pitching Taima to the ground as he struggled to pull the barb from his flesh. But it was too late.

Almost immediately, he felt the effects of the poison coursing through his system. He knew there was no antidote. He jerked at the barbed arrow, felt it rip through his flesh. He couldn't get it free. He felt himself losing strength.

The scene began to spin slowly. Onawa screamed in a rage, chattering from a long distance away. A knife glittered and sliced through his shoulder. The pain coursed through him, but it was no longer his body. He opened his mouth to shout about Inteus, how he was leading a host of men with rifles up the secret path to kill the villagers. His mouth would not open. His voice would not respond. He felt a coldness creep along all his limbs, and he wondered if he were going to die.

Onawa was still screaming from a great distance. The ground spun, and the rocks jounced up and down. He was being carried along the path, hoisted high by the Havasupai braves. Darkness, sky, rocks, trees, and a village. Two gigantic columns of rock like two guardian gods stood over the small wickiups. The tall rocks bent down, and there were scowling faces. One was Inteus. The other was Cavell Barnes. Fargo struggled again to shout out the news, but he was paralyzed. His body would not respond to his commands. Again and again, he tried. He could barely keep his eyes open.

If he did not tell them, they would all be slaughtered. If he did not tell them, they would all die. The words beat into his brain like a drumbeat. Sweat poured from him, heat and more heat. Darkness. Drums. Sweat. Where was he?

"Toholwa." He heard the word. *"Toholwa."*

He felt himself bathed in heat, his head reeling. Where the arrow had entered his shoulder, someone was holding something hot. The air was hot, blasting hot. He tried to speak again, found he could just move his tongue. He was in the sweat lodge, he knew. They were trying to sweat the poison out of him.

He commanded his finger to move and found that it did, a little. His eyelids weighed more than Taima had. He forced them open, saw the darkness, chinks of light. Turned his head to see a dark figure, an old man, bending over a pitch-covered basket. With two sticks, the old man dropped a stone into the basket and steam rose in a cloud. The old man repeated the motion again. Fargo closed his eyes and felt the sweat pour from him.

His throat burned. Someone lifted his heavy head, forced open his mouth, and poured a stream of cool liquid down his throat. He sputtered, struggled to swallow, choked, then managed it. He drank deeply, gratefully, then fell into the heat and darkness again.

The sound of a rattle woke him, chanting and the hiss of steam. He opened his eyes, felt his tongue swollen in his mouth, licked his dry lips. He forced his mouth open, willed his voice to speak. He rasped, incoherent at first.

"Inteus. Comes. Bad. Men." These were the words he remembered in their tongue. The rattling stopped abruptly, and there was silence in the dark sweat lodge.

"Inteus. Comes. Bad. Men."

Some of the men murmured among themselves. The rattle started up, then stopped. Fargo summoned his strength, then slowly he sat up. His body scarcely obeyed him. It was hard to move, his joints felt stiff and his skin numb. The muscles seemed not to understand what he wanted them to do. He spoke the words again. This time the old man stepped forward and spoke a stream of incomprehensible words.

"I am Skye Fargo," he forced himself to answer in English. "White man. Anybody speak white man tongue?" His words were slurred with the effort. At his name and the sound of the white man's speech, they muttered in surprise.

"You are not river god?" the old man said in English. There was a shocked silence inside the sweat lodge.

"No!" Fargo almost shouted. The paralysis was

subsiding. "Inteus is leading a bunch of men here. Now. To attack the village. To kill every last one of you. Send your men out to the secret path. There's not a moment to lose. Now!"

But even as he spoke, the sound of gunfire erupted from a distance away. The old man shouted in the Havasupai tongue, and they pushed out of the sweat lodge. He was left alone in the near darkness. With a mighty effort Fargo swung his feet over the edge of the ledge and forced himself to stand up. He swayed back and forth and had to grab ahold of a beam in the wall or else he would have toppled over.

But he'd given the alarm too late. Outside, he heard the sound of firing, the screams of the Havasupai Indians as they were murdered, the shouts of Cavell Barnes and his men.

And a moment later the hulking form of a man appeared in the lighted door of the sweat lodge. Fargo recognized Platan Arnez. Summoning every ounce of will, with a cry of fury, he forced his body forward, barreling into the gigantic man.

7

The huge hulk of Platan Arnez stood in the doorway of the sweat lodge, his lanks of greasy hair hanging to his shoulders and the buckskin thong around his low forehead. He blinked his eyes trying to see into the darkness of the sweat lodge.

Fargo barreled straight into him, knocking him clean off his feet. The two tumbled into the sunlight outside. Arnez seemed momentarily dazed by the sudden attack as Fargo pummeled him with his powerful fists, fighting the lethargy and weakness that the poison arrow had left in his body.

He delivered a swift uppercut to Arnez's jaw, then a hard left into his belly. The big man rolled over to escape the onslaught of Fargo's blows. Arnez was fighting one-armed, having been winged by Fargo's bullet but his right arm was still powerful. Arnez lashed out, and Fargo felt the pain radiate from his midsection as the big man's fist drove into him.

Arnez shook his head, and his eyes cleared. He focused on Fargo's face, recognizing him at last and fury danced in his eyes. Fargo gave him no chance to follow through. Thinking of Dofield and his ranch and all the trouble the Barnes gang had caused, Fargo felt the rage pour into his arm. With all his strength, he delivered a right into Arnez's hard jaw that snapped his head to the side and made his eyes roll back. The huge man shuddered, then lay back unconscious.

Fargo got heavily to his feet, his head spinning as much from the lingering effects of the poison as from the blows. The scene was spinning slightly around him. And then he realized he was not alone.

They were there, all of them. Barnes' men stood in a wide circle around him, their rifles in hand. Fargo glanced around the village. On the ground between the small wickiups lay many bodies of Havasupai. Barnes and his men had been merciless.

A short distance away, Fargo saw a crowd of Indians huddled together in the center of a sheep corral. Two of the men were guarding them with drawn rifles. If any of the Indians took a step toward the fence, one of the men would fire a bullet. In an instant Fargo saw the whole story of what had happened while he had been in the sweat lodge. The village had been overtaken. None of the Havasupai braves had remained guarding the pathway but had been with everyone else outside the sweat lodge, anxiously awaiting news of what they thought was the fallen river god. And when Barnes and his men came storming up the pathway, led by Inteus, they hadn't had their poison arrows close to hand. He could see the Havasupai crowded together in the pen anxiously looking in his direction to try to understand what was happening. On their faces were expressions of confusion, of anger, of disbelief. Among them he spotted the old man and the young girl named Onawa.

"So the big hero, the Trailsman, turns up again," Barnes smirked as he stepped forward. "Where's the little blond chick?"

Fargo shrugged nonchalantly.

"Never mind," Barnes said. "We'll track her down later." He sneered and exchanged glances with Potter, who stood nearby, a mean expression on his face. Barnes suddenly brought up his rifle barrel to cover Fargo. In an instant the Colt was in Fargo's hand. He aimed at a point between Barnes' eyes. The rest of the gang suddenly brought up their rifles, too, and a long moment passed. They all knew that if they shot at him, he'd pull the trigger and blast Barnes. What they didn't know was that the Colt was waterlogged and useless. It was a standoff.

Inteus appeared, walking between the wickiups. His hard face was stony with the satisfied expression of one who has at last gained a long-desired revenge. He looked around the village of his tribe contemptuously, his lip curling. Then he spotted Fargo and halted in surprise.

"So you've come back to the Havasupai village to betray your own people," Fargo said. True to form, Inteus only stared at him and refused to answer. "I hear you're going to show them where all the tribe's gold is hidden."

"How you hear . . ." he began, looking suspiciously at Barnes. The gray–haired man turned and stared at Potter, who looked guilty as all hell.

"They threatened to burn me," Potter protested. "That bastard's redskin brother was going to fry me alive. I didn't tell him much—"

"Potter told me everything," Fargo cut in. He holstered his Colt, and the men slowly lowered their rifle barrels. "Yeah, I know the whole story. I've known about it for years. There's a treasury of gold hidden in this canyon so big it'll make every one of you men richer than Solomon." He saw the gleam of desire in the expressions of Barnes and all his men.

"He made me tell—" Potter protested.

"Potter also told me Inteus is going to show you where the gold is," Fargo added. "So, Inteus, where is it?"

Inteus looked nervous for a moment, then hardened his expression.

"All of tribe must die first. All Havasupai dead. Then tell. This is deal with white men."

Fargo knew what Inteus' game was. As soon as Inteus had his revenge and every Havasupai man, woman, and child was killed, he was planning to lead Barnes and his men on a wild-goose chase after a cache of gold that never even existed. And then, at some point, he would simply vanish.

"You trust a redskin?" Fargo asked Barnes conspiratorially. "If I were you, I'd put first things first.

Get your hands on that gold right now. Then you can take care of the dirty work. I'd make sure the gold is really there."

A glimmer of suspicion flickered across Barnes' face. He stared at Inteus, then back at Fargo.

"So, where is the gold?" Barnes said impatiently.

"All tribe killed first," Inteus said stubbornly.

Fargo raised his eyebrows at Barnes as if to say you couldn't trust an Indian. Barnes was falling for the act.

"I want to get that gold *now*," Barnes said. "We'll take care of business afterward."

"No!" Inteus said. "Kill first. Then gold."

Barnes' face turned bright red with fury.

"I say I want that gold now." He shifted his aim toward Inteus. The Indian saw he had no choice, but still he hesitated.

"No," he repeated.

"You just can't trust a redskin," Fargo said to Barnes.

"If I'm going to trust you, you'll have to hand over your gun," Barnes countered.

"Fair enough," Fargo said. The waterlogged Colt wasn't doing him any good anyway. He drew and handed it butt first to Barnes, who stuck it in his belt.

"I know how to find the gold. That brother of Inteus, Taima, told me." Inteus stared back at him, knowing he was lying but unable to accuse him without admitting the gold didn't even exist. Fargo's thoughts ran ahead, and a plan began to take shape. He remembered hearing about the path that led up to the canyon rim and the desert lands above. And also about another route, a crack in the rock where the Havasupai of old had climbed up to escape when the tribe was under attack. If he could just get Barnes and his men into that crevice, he would have a fighting chance.

"Why *should* I trust you, Trailsman?" Barnes said.

"Because we'll strike a bargain. And I always stick to my bargains. I find the gold, I go free. Simple. And you don't have to deal with this slippery redskin anymore."

Barnes considered the offer with interest, but he was wary, expecting a trick. Platan Arnez had come around a few minutes before and had sat listening to their conversation. Now he got to his feet.

"You ain't gonna believe this Trailsman, are you?" Arnez said. He spat in Fargo's direction.

"Either him or the redskin," Barnes said thoughtfully. Platan Arnez pulled at his greasy locks and stared at Fargo mistrustfully as he stroked his bruised jaw.

"But, boss—" Platan complained.

"Shut up," Cavell Barnes snapped. Barnes clearly did not tolerate any opinions from his men. He narrowed his eyes and seemed to suddenly make up his mind. "Okay, Fargo. Let's see you find that gold. And now."

"Bring me the young girl from the corral," Fargo instructed. "The one named Onawa. I can get her to lead us. And bring the old man, too. To translate."

"Now, wait a minute. I thought you said you knew where the gold was," Barnes spat back.

"Just listen," Fargo said. "If you don't like the way things are going, you can kill me and deal with him again." He jerked his thumb toward Inteus.

"He's lying!" Inteus shouted, "He doesn't know where the gold is! Only *I* know where."

"Bullshit," Fargo said. "Your brother knew, too. The whole tribe knows." Barnes stepped closer to Inteus and stared the Indian in the face.

"I don't trust you, redskin," Barnes said. "I didn't trust you from the first time I laid eyes on you." He stepped away and spoke to Fargo. "I don't trust you, either, Trailsman. But if this goddamn redskin won't take us to the treasure, let's see you find that gold. Now. Right now."

It was working, Fargo thought as he tried to keep the expression of relief from his face. Potter walked over to the corral and dragged Onawa back with him. She looked defiant, but underneath he knew she was scared. The old man followed, dragging a wounded leg behind him. His eyes were as still and calm as deep liquid pools. The men called out as they watched the girl being brought forward.

"Hey, boss, can't we have a little fun here?"

"Can't we do the pretty ones before we shoot 'em?"

"Shut up," Barnes snapped, his mind on the gold. He stepped up to listen, suspicious.

"You will translate my words to Havasupai tongue," Fargo said in English to the old man. "Tell the girl to take us to get the gold. Taima said the gold is hidden in the crack in the rock, the secret passage up to the desert." The old man held his gaze for a brief instant and an understanding passed between them.

"They're trying to trick you," Inteus said hotly.

"So *you* tell us where the gold is," Fargo shot at him.

Inteus fell silent.

"The gold is up there," Fargo said, pointing halfway up to the lip of the canyon.

Barnes was following his every word and gesture. "In this secret passageway. Tell Onawa to lead me to the passageway and the gold, or everyone will be killed."

The old man nodded gravely and spoke to Onawa in Havasupai. She looked surprised at first, and it took her longer to catch on. She was not as wise as the old man, not as practiced at hiding her true thoughts. But she did not ask any questions, only nodded her head silently to indicate her willingness to lead them to the secret passageway through the rock cleft. When the old man finished speaking, Barnes turned to Inteus.

"So you understand this Indian talk. What did he tell her? Are they up to something?"

"No," Inteus said after a pause. Inteus knew Fargo was lying. And he knew that the old man was playing along, understanding that they must make a show of leading Barnes and his gang until a moment when they could overcome them. Inteus had apparently changed his tactics. He obviously had something else up his sleeve, too.

"Well, let's get a move on," Fargo said to Barnes.

"You'd better leave two of your men to watch over those Havasupai." A quarrel broke out among the men as to who would have to stay and do guard duty. Everybody wanted to come along and get his hands on the gold as soon as possible. Barnes finally settled it by leaving Arnez and another man behind. Potter's face was fairly beaming as he thought of the gold. Inteus tried to remain behind, too, but Barnes grabbed him by the neck of his buckskins and insisted he accompany them.

It was an awkward party. Barnes and the four remaining men were all armed to the teeth. Inteus carried a long knife and brought up the rear. Barnes insisted that the girl go first, followed by Fargo. He drew his rifle and planted it between his shoulder blades.

"No tricks, Trailsman," Barnes said.

"No tricks," he agreed, hoping Barnes wouldn't stumble and kill him accidentally.

Onawa's lithe form went ahead of them, agilely ascending a rocky path that led between chokecherry bushes and a few cottonwood trees. The sky was blue overhead, the sun shone down, and the wind rustled in the leaves. In moments they were walking in the shadow along the base of a mammoth cliff.

"Where the hell are we going?" Barnes growled impatiently.

"It's just ahead," Fargo said confidently, even though he had no idea where the rock cleft path began.

After a moment Onawa stopped and pointed upward. In the smooth red rock that rose above them were carved small hand and footholds which ascended upward.

"One of you go first," Barnes directed. Potter nervously climbed up as they waited below. In another minute he called down.

"Yeah, there's a kind of cave up here."

"That's it!" Fargo exclaimed, trying to get the men excited. As they climbed the rock one by one up to the cave, he started to fabricate stories about the supposed rich lode of gold.

"These Havasupai have been knocking over every stagecoach and bank delivery in these parts for years. Only nobody could ever catch 'em at it. There's more gold here than in the U.S. Treasury. Gold coins, gold bars, gold ingots, gold jewelry, the whole thing."

Fargo could tell that Barnes, Potter, and the two other men were getting stirred up. They were impatient to get to the top of the rock and tried to get by each other. Once he climbed over the top, Fargo saw that his plan was going to work.

They were standing on the lip of a cave overlooking the small canyon of the Havasupai. At the back of the cave was a deep crack, a crevice that ran through the solid rock that rose hundreds of feet above them to the top of the butte. This secret way out of the canyon meant climbing up through solid rock. And they would have to go single file. Onawa gestured toward the cleft questioningly.

"Taima told me it's right up there," Fargo said, pointing upward.

He could almost hear Barnes and his men panting with greed. Inteus followed in sullen silence, and Fargo wondered when he'd make his move. Barnes and his men had almost forgotten their caution in their desire to get their hands on the gold. Barnes slung his rifle over his shoulder and peered upward, through the half-light.

"Oh, boy," Potter said, rubbing his hands together. "A life of women and whiskey."

Barnes insisted Onawa climb up first, followed by Fargo and then himself. The girl began climbing gracefully, and Fargo followed. He waited until all the men were ascending. He looked back and saw below him, in the dim light that filtered down from above through the crevice, the line of men clinging to the rock, making their slow way like ants crawling upward.

"How much farther?" Barnes growled.

"Right up here," Fargo said. Ahead he saw a small ledge. He pushed Onawa onto it, out of the line of fire, then paused as if to take a breath. He waited until Barnes had nearly caught up, then he suddenly reached over and grabbed the barrel of the rifle, wrenching it around.

Barnes cried out in surprise, almost losing his grip on the rock. He tried to grab the rifle, but couldn't. Instead, his finger brushed the trigger and the gun discharged, filling the cleft with an explosion that deafened them. The bullet whined, ricocheted off the stone walls, and rock chips showered them. The men below shouted.

Fargo kicked downward but missed, and Barnes fumbled at his belt, then drew Fargo's Colt.

"Damn you, Trailsman," he shouted. He pulled the trigger, but the waterlogged gun only clicked. He pulled it again and again, then tried to throw it upward. But Fargo wrenched the rifle free from Barnes, then kicked out again, a blow that planted his boot firmly in the man's face. Barnes grappled for a handhold for a moment, lost it, then plummeted downward, sliding and bouncing down between the rock walls, smashing into Potter climbing behind him, then into the next man and the next. Fargo reversed the rifle and fired, once, twice, again, again, again, and the rocks trembled, a shower of stones fell down on top of the men. He stopped. It was quiet below. He was sure he'd plugged Barnes, Potter, and the other man. But he wasn't sure about Inteus. Hopefully, the other men falling on top of him had killed him, too.

Onawa stood terrified and pressed against the wall of the ledge. A small shower of stones rained down on him, and he hoped there wouldn't be a cave-in.

"Come on!" he shouted. Onawa led him on quickly and in a few seconds, they emerged into the air. They stood on a promontory overlooking the Havasupai canyon. Down below there came the sound of two gunshots, then shouts and cries. Over the tops of the cottonwood trees, Fargo could see the village and the sheep corral.

He watched as several of the Havasupai threw themselves at the two guards and had been shot dead. But before Barnes' men could fire again, they had been overrun by the rest of the tribe. Now the corral was a tangle of bodies, and it looked like the Indians were wreaking their revenge on the two men who had terrorized them.

Just then he spotted a figure running along the edge of the canyon, trying to stay undercover. It was Inteus, heading for the escape route, the path back down to the Grand Canyon. Fargo swore and left her, hurriedly climbing back down through the cleft, skittering over the stone, almost falling, determined not to let Inteus escape.

At the bottom was a pile of stones and broken bodies of the men. Cavell Barnes lay on top, his eyes open and blank. The other men were beneath him, a tangle of legs and arms and shattered stone. He had to squeeze around them to get out. Then he climbed the last small cliff and ran, pounding the earth, ran faster than he'd ever run, the bushes tearing at him, his breath ragged and gasping, running, running, flashing through the village as the Indians called to him, then on toward the entrance of the path.

A small figure up ahead was crossing the shallow creek right above the waterfall. It was Inteus. Fargo ran full speed, and Inteus turned when he heard him approach, pulled his long knife, and crouched down, his narrow eyes like black fire.

Rage, the black rage of the unrevenged deaths, the unavenged wrongs that Inteus had committed, rose in Fargo until it blotted out everything but the figure of the man standing before him. With a cry he sprang forward, everything forgotten but the setting right of all the wrongs. And he saw fear in the face of Inteus. Fargo's powerful hand closed around the Indian's wrist and squeezed harder than he ever had. The knife dropped into the stream. Inteus took a step backward as Fargo, the fury welling in him like hot fire in every vein, advanced, lashing out again and again. As if from a distance, he heard the sound of the falling water, saw the precipice behind Inteus as he came on, pressing the man farther, farther, until finally with a final lunge, he barreled into him.

Inteus took a step backward, his foot slid on a rock and he teetered, then fell backward into space, falling, falling, as if in slow motion down beside the long ribbon of blue water as it fell almost two hundred feet. Fargo grasped a boulder and looked down as the body of Inteus landed on a rock and lay still, far far below.

He straightened up and looked down into the valley below where Havasu Creek wound between the red cliffs toward where it would soon join the Big Colorado River. The red tumbled rocks and green grass seemed eternal, unchangeable, as did the white majestic clouds that slowly moved above in the blue sky. It was time to get back to the village, help with the burying of the dead. He'd get Ed Dofield's money out of Cavill Barnes' pockets. Then he had to find Paulina again.

Suddenly, he caught a movement below in the canyon. He stared and saw two small figures climbing the hillside. The sun reflected a hint of gold. Fargo laughed.

There was no telling how Paulina Parker and Bishy had found their way down the river and up the Havasu Creek. Maybe they'd built a raft of driftwood and then seen the boats Barnes had undoubtedly abandoned at the mouth of the creek. Or maybe she'd just got lucky. But however it was, Paulina Parker had made it this far in one piece. She stopped, looked up at the falls, and apparently spotted him, there, a small figure standing on top. She began to wave.

Yeah, however she'd made it this far, Fargo thought, he was sure he'd hear all about it. Or read it in one of her books someday. He started down the path to meet them.

LOOKING FORWARD!
The following is the opening
section from the next novel in the exciting
Trailsman **series from Signet:**

THE TRAILSMAN #182
BLOOD CANYON

Montana, 1860. The early Mexican explorers
named it the land of the mountains. The Ameri-
can pioneers knew it as the land cradled by the
towering Rocky Mountains, and there were
some who wanted to make the evils of another
time and another place come alive again . . .

It would have been just another stagecoach to the
ordinary observer as it rolled across the Montana
Territory. But the big man astride the magnificent
Ovaro was not the ordinary observer. Some knew
him as Skye Fargo, others knew him simply as the
Trailsman, the man who combined experience, instinct, and a special awareness to see where others
only looked, to detect what ordinary men missed
seeing. His lake-blue eyes were narrowed as he
watched the stage move along the road. "Something's not right," he muttered to himself. "I don't
like it." He moved the horse forward, out of the
trees where the sun made the Ovaro's jet-black

fore-and-hind quarters glisten in contrast to the gleaming white midsection.

He hadn't had any luck so far, he reminded himself grimly as he thought about the reason that had brought him into northwest Montana Territory. Perhaps things were about to change, he hoped. But his eyes went to the line of rocky hills that ran along the far side of the road. The half-dozen riders disappeared behind a line of tall rocks but not before he caught a glimpse of them. They had been riding almost all afternoon in the high hills, almost paralleling the stage and holding a steady pace as they moved through the high rocks. It was impossible to tell whether they were watching the stage or just passing the same way, but Fargo decided to stop the stagecoach, regardless, and spurred the Ovaro forward. He quickly caught up to the stage and saw it was no mud wagon with a light-framed top and roll-down canvas windows but a full Concord coach with a straight-grained white ash frame, side panels of poplar, and running gear of strong white oak.

The lone driver turned in the driver's box to look at him as he came alongside and Fargo saw a leathery face with a black beard and dark eyes under a worn, floppy-brimmed hat. "Rein up, friend," Fargo called, and the man pulled the two teams to a halt.

"Nothing to rob," the driver said.

"Didn't come to do any robbing," Fargo said, and drew closer to the stage. He peered inside at three fabric-covered seats that could hold nine passengers, and his glance swept the floor as well. But he saw no blood stains, no bullet holes, no marks of trouble, and he returned his eyes to the driver, who stayed sitting quietly. "Thought you might be in trouble," Fargo said. "I've never seen a big Concord traveling this country without passengers." He paused as his eyes swept the roof rack. "No luggage, either, not even a strong box." He moved the Ovaro forward and lifted the black canvas to look inside the front boot, then did the same with the long slope of the rear boot. "Nothing anywhere," he grunted. "What would make a company send out a big Concord completely empty?"

"The stage was a special charter," the driver said. "Paid for by six gents, up from Wyoming. They paid enough to cover the trip back empty."

Fargo let his face show that he was impressed as he took in the stage again, the body barn red, the wheels yellow, and the name of the builder in black letters along the bottom of the body, Abbot, Downing & Co. Concord, New Hampshire. It was a real Concord, unquestionably, and the driver's explanation seemed reasonable. But not satisfying, Fargo grunted. He'd never heard of a stage line that wouldn't try to fill up their coach even if they'd been paid enough to make a run back empty. Stagecoach owners didn't turn away from making a double profit. He moved the pinto slowly around the big coach and silently cursed as he saw nothing that suggested any explanation other than the driver had offered. But there was something wrong. He felt it with that sixth sense that seldom failed him.

"Who owns the stage?" he asked.

"Mullevy Brothers. They do short-line charters," the driver said.

"Never heard of them," Fargo said.

"They're new," the driver said.

Fargo nodded and backed the Ovaro from the stage. "Glad you weren't in any trouble," he said.

"Glad you weren't a damn road bandit." The driver sniffed, snapped the reins, and drove away. Fargo tossed a quick glance up at the hills. The riders had gone their way or they were behind the tall rocks, and Fargo moved the pinto slowly along the road. He let the coach roll out of sight as he followed along the road and saw the sun going down over the tops of the Little Belt mountains. Another hour would bring night, he guessed, and made a wager with himself that the stage wouldn't be driving by dark. He kept the pinto almost at a walk as he followed along the road, scanning the high rocks occasionally without glimpsing the six riders. But they could well be unseen amid the jagged rock formations, he knew, and soon the blue-gray of dusk rolled down from the mountains. Dissatisfaction continued to ride with him. There was something more to the empty stage, he told himself again, though he had to wonder if he was just desperate for a lead that wouldn't prove empty.

He hadn't found himself riding this lonely road for pleasure, he reminded himself, though Paula Hodges still remained a goal and that would spell pleasure. He pushed aside thoughts of Paula and increased the Ovaro's pace as dusk slid into darkness.

He'd gone another half hour when flickering lights broke the stygian blackness of the night, and he finally found himself riding up to three flat-roofed buildings that were plainly a way station. He reined up in front of the largest of the buildings where a weathered sign, TRAVELER'S WAY STATION, hung from the top edge of the roof. He scanned the scene and failed to see the stagecoach. His eyes moved along a hitching post, expecting to find six horses, but he saw only two, both already unsaddled. Dismounting, he left the Ovaro at the hitching post and walked around to the rear of the building, where a thin smile touched his face as he saw the big Concord there, horses unhitched, undoubtedly in the nearby barn.

He walked back to the main building and went inside to find a big log-paneled room with three long dining tables and heavy wooden chairs. A woman in a blouse and skirt, middle-aged with a worn face, cleared dishes from one of the long tables and glanced up at him. A small man came forward, olive-skinned with black hair in need of cutting and small eyes, and quickly offered the edgy obsequiousness of a small-time innkeeper. "Welcome, my friend," he said, and Fargo was surprised to hear a Mexican accent. "A good meal, a good bed, or both?" he added.

"Both," Fargo said. "With a shot of bourbon."

The man spread his hands apologetically. "No bourbon, my friend, but I have good rye whiskey, Old Overholt."

"That'll do," Fargo said, and the man gestured to the woman .

"I am Santo. Welcome to my little inn," the man said. He turned to the wall behind him and lifted a large key from a rack and handed it to Fargo. "Room three. Down the hall."

"Not too busy tonight," Fargo commented. "I saw only two horses outside."

The man shrugged. "We are never too busy."

"I saw six riders earlier, thought they might be heading this way," Fargo remarked as the man poured a shot glass of rye.

"They have not stopped here," Santos said with an air of resigned acceptance.

"I'll bring my saddle in," Fargo said, and hurried to the Ovaro, returning in minutes carrying the saddle. He went to room three and found it small, spare, but clean, made up of a single bed, a battered dresser, a water basin, and a lamp. When he finished freshening up, he went outside to find the woman serving a plate of corned antelope and potatoes that was surprisingly tasty. He had just finished the meal when the stage driver came into the room to ask for a pitcher of water. Seeing Fargo, surprise flooded his face, then apprehension. "This one of your regular stops?" Fargo asked cheerfully.

"No," the driver said curtly, and hurried from the room with his pitcher. Fargo downed the last of the rye, and the woman cleared away the dishes. The innkeeper disappeared into the back of the inn with her. Silence and two candles were Fargo's companions as he waited a little longer before going outside into the warm night. He strolled to the rear of the inn and the stagecoach, where, in the light of a half-moon, he examined the coach again, paying special attention to the front and rear boot. But he found nothing and returned to the little room in the building, where he undressed and stretched out on the bed as a warm breeze came through the single window. With his eyes closed, the sight of the big Concord rolling empty across the rich Montana Territory floated through his thoughts. Anyone else would have paid it no heed, he knew, a big Concord rolling its way. But his sixth sense continued to prod him. That and the frustration that had become a larger companion each day, and he let the events that had brought him to the Montana Territory unfold again in his thoughts.

Roy Averson had contacted him through Dave Landers only a few days after he'd found a new cattle trail for Dave all the way up from the Colorado Territory into lower Montana. The meeting had taken place in a small town just north of Yellowstone, where Averson had waited inside an empty shed with only a table and two chairs as furniture. Roy Averson turned out to be a big man with salt-and-pepper hair, a strong face with bushy black eyebrows, and the piercing eyes of an eagle. He had a commanding presence, almost lordly, with a deep voice and broad gestures, as though he more properly belonged in another century. The impression was immediately heightened by three objects lying on a piece of burlap on the table, which Fargo quickly recognized from pictures he had seen. Averson was quick to see the moment mirrored in Fargo's eyes. "You know something about medieval weaponry, Fargo?" he asked.

"Not a lot," Fargo said.

"We'll have time to talk about that at a later date. Now we'll concentrate on why I asked to see you," Roy Averson said. He drew a thick stack of bills from his pocket and thumped the money down on the table. "That's all yours, Fargo. Dave Landers said you're the very best. That's what I need, and I'm willing to pay for the very best."

Fargo's quick glance at the stack of bills told him there had to be at least two thousand dollars there. "What do you expect for that kind of money?" he questioned.

"I'm expecting you to find my granddaughter and bring her back to me," Averson said. "They grabbed her with two of my hands when they all went to pick up a Welsh Cob I bought her. My fault. I should never have let her go to get the damn pony."

"Any ideas who?"

"Kidnappers, that's who. I'm expecting a ransom note any day," Roy Averson thundered. "They had to lay low with her for a spell, hide out someplace, because they knew I'd have my men scouring the whole damn countryside for them."

"I take it you did that," Fargo said.

"And found nothing. That's when I came looking for you. They'll be moving her. They can't sit around here, where I'll find them sooner or later. This is the best chance to find her before they hide her away someplace. The child's life is at stake. God knows what could happen to her on purpose or accidentally."

"But you haven't had a ransom note yet," Fargo said.

"That'll come. That's just a formality. They know I'll pay anything to get the child," Roy Averson said.

"How old is she?" Fargo asked.

"Ten. She's small and blond, and her name is Amy," Averson said. "From what I hear, if there's a trail to be picked up or a blade of grass out of place, you'll find it and that's what I want you to do. Find something that'll lead you to her."

"You have any leads?" Fargo asked.

"A few. I'll give them to you. The important thing

is that I'm sure she hasn't been moved yet. I've had almost a roadblock around the entire area."

Fargo let a wry sound escape his lips. "You'd need a hell of a lot more men than you have to seal off the whole region," he said. Roy Averson's mouth tightened. "You're right, of course," the man grunted, putting one hand on the stack of bills. "This is yours. I'll give you as to use to buy information. Cold cash goes a long way to loosen tongues."

Fargo's lips pursed as he thought. He had written Paula Hodges he'd come visiting soon as he finished the job for Dave Landers and was there in Montana Territory. It was a promise he very much wanted to keep. Paula would be full of waiting passion, and she was too good an old friend and too rewarding a lover to disappoint. Yet he had a little cushion of time before he was expected, and Averson was offering the kind of money only a fool would turn down. Yet there was more, he admitted with an inner wince. He hated to put passion on hold for anything. It was against his principles. But a little girl's life was possibly at stake, and that took precedence over money, passion, or whatever. A long sigh escaped him as he turned to Roy Averson.

"Where do I contact you if I find her?" Fargo asked, and saw the man's commanding face take on more satisfaction than gratitude.

"My own property is way up northwest Montana, a place called Blood Canyon. But I figure they'll be moving through this area, and I want to stay close. I've set up quarters in a town called Cutter's Bend, at the inn there." Averson said.

"I know the place," Fargo nodded.

"Contact me there, hopefully with Amy," Roy Averson said.

"Let's hear what leads you have," Fargo said, and Averson quickly told him what few leads he had gathered. They had little substance, Fargo noted inwardly.

"I'll be waiting at Cutter's Bend, Fargo. I know you won't disappoint me," Averson said.

Fargo remembered how the man's words proved to be more wishful thinking than realistic as, in the days that followed, he pursued each of the leads, only to find then dissipate into nothing. He thought back to the last one, which had seemed the most promising, a saloon in a miserable little town of a handful of rotting buildings. Someone had seen a man stop there and leave a little girl tied in the saddle of a horse tethered outside. When he visited the saloon, Fargo recalled, he had announced to everyone within earshot his willingness to pay hard cash to find the girl. There had been the usual murmur that disclaimed any knowledge until a short man sidled up to where Fargo leaned against the bar.

"I might know where there's a kid," he said. "I could find out."

"That'd be good." Fargo said carefully.

"How will I know if she's the right one?" the man asked, craftiness in his face.

"I'll go with you," Fargo replied.

"No way. I tell you if she's the right one, you give me my money, and I'm gone. I don't wait around for you to change your mind," the man said. "She got a name?"

Fargo took in the man's shifty-eyed face. Everything about him was run-down, from his frayed shirt collar to his worn clothes. Yet he fit. The information Fargo wanted wouldn't be coming from upstanding citizens. "Her name's Amy," Fargo said. "She's small and blond."

"How much?" the man insisted.

"A thousand," Fargo said, deciding to make it something the man would be happy to get. "If she's the right one."

"I'll be back," the man said.

"When?" Fargo asked sharply.

"This time tomorrow," the man said.

"I'll be here," Fargo said. "You've a name, mister?"

"Willie Smith," the man said, and Fargo watched him hurry from the saloon. His eyes scanned the others at the bar.

"Anybody else see the little girl left outside?" he asked.

"I did," a gray-bearded man said, and Fargo grunted. At least Willie Smith hadn't been the only one to see the child. There had been a little girl held on a horse, and Fargo allowed himself a glimmer of hope. This lead was showing more substance than any of the others, and he finished his drink and left the saloon. He bedded down in a clump of ash and was waiting back in the saloon when Willie Smith appeared. The man hurried to him, licking his lips nervously.

"She's the kid you want," he said.

"Where is she?" Fargo questioned sharply.

"Not so fast. My money first. You could get her and not pay up," Willie Smith said.

"And you could have the wrong kid or be making up the whole thing," Fargo said. "Who's got her?"

"Don't know exactly, but they're keeping her in a shack," the man said. "I know where the shack is."

"How many are there?" Fargo pressed.

Willie Smith licked his lips again, and his hands twitched nervously. "They're keeping her alone."

"'No guards?" Fargo frowned.

"They don't want to call attention to her," Smith said.

Fargo cursed inwardly. He wanted to reject Willie Smith's answer. It was entirely too convenient. Yet it was just plausible enough to be true. "I still won't buy a pig in a poke, he said. "Take me to the shack. If it's the right kid, you'll get your money. That's as far as I'll go," Fargo said.

Willie Smith spat on the floor, a gesture of anger and unhappy realization. "Let's go," he muttered, and Fargo followed him from the saloon. He rose a few paces behind Willie Smith as the man rode north and down into a small dip in the land. After another fifteen minutes of riding, Fargo saw the shack, standing alone, no horses tied outside it, no figures standing guard. "She's inside," Willie Smith said as he came to a halt. Fargo drew up and swung to the ground, raising the Colt as he approached the shack. Willie Smith dismounted and hurried after him. A lone window let Fargo peer in, where a candle gave enough light for him to see the inside of a shack. A little girl sat on a hard-back chair, ankles and wrists bound, her hair falling just below her ears on both sides of her face. There was nothing else in the shack except bits and pieces of broken boxes and general litter. The child wore a shapeless one-piece dress that covered her knees.

"I'll take my money," Willie Smith said as Fargo moved to the door of the shack.

"You'll wait," Fargo grunted, opened the door, and stepped inside the shack. The little girl rose from the chair at once. "Easy, honey. No one's going to hurt you," Fargo said as he walked toward the child. She seemed the right age, Fargo observed, her face smudged with dirt, her eyes wide, frightened. He halted beside her, his eyes moving across hair, a bright, fresh yellow. "What's your name, sweetie?" he asked.

"Amy," the child said, and he peered at the dirt smudges on her face again, lowered his gaze to her bare arms, where there were more smudges of dirt. He brushed his fingers across her left arm. The streaks of dirt didn't come away. They had been there long enough to harden, and he noticed more dirt smudges on her legs. His eyes went to the child's hair again, and he touched the bright yellow shine of it. His lips formed a grim smile.

"You want to give me the money now?" Willie Smith said truculently. His eyes widened as he saw the Colt in Fargo's hand.

"How about I shoot your knee cap off instead?" Fargo asked.

"What's wrong with you?" Willie Smith frowned.

"I don't like to be taken," Fargo said, saw the small pitcher of water beside the chair, and picked it up. With a quick motion he poured it over the little girl's hair. The child gave a tiny shudder as the water hit her, but she didn't move. Fargo watched as it took only moments before part of her blond hair developed streaks of brown. "Amateur job," Fargo bit out. "Probably peroxide with nothing else to hold it."

He turned to Willie Smith, his eyes blue ice. "How'd you know?" Smith asked.

"You should have cleaned her up all over," Fargo said. "You take her off some nearby farm?" The man's truculent silence was an answer. "You saw a chance to make some money and jumped at it," Fargo went on. "You did a quick job on her hair to produce a kid to fit the one I'm looking for. Did you really think you could pull it off?" Again, silence was his answer as Willie Smith shifted his feet uncomfortably. "Take her home and get out of my sight before I lose my temper," Fargo rasped and strode from the shack.

It had ended there, another lead that, despite its early promise, had frittered into nothing, and Fargo turned the thoughts off in his mind as he lay on the bed. Since the last lead had unraveled, the frustration had grown stronger, and he realized that when he spotted the stagecoach he was alert for anything that caught his eye. The empty stage still jabbed at him as he lay on the bed. Somehow, somewhere, there was something wrong, he told himself again before he drew sleep around himself and let the night go its silent way.

He woke with the morning and allowed himself the luxury of the bed for a little while longer before he swung to his feet and used the washbasin. He heard the sounds of the stage horses being hitched as he dressed and decided to leave his saddle in the room as he went down for breakfast. He walked along the hallway of the inn when he heard Santo talking, then the voice of the stage driver. "That is for the extra dinner and the extra bottle of water, *señor*," Santo said.

"All right, here," the driver grunted, and Fargo heard the sounds of the coins being spilled onto the table. He stayed back against the wall of the corridor and heard the driver hurry from the inn. Moments later, he heard the big Concord pulling away from the inn, and he stepped from the corridor into the main room. The woman brought him a mug of strong coffee, which he downed with long sips as Santo returned.

"Good morning, *señor*," the innkeeper said cheerfully.

"I heard the stage driver pay you for an extra dinner," Fargo said. "Why would a man order two dinners and extra water?"

The innkeeper shrugged. "Maybe he was very hungry and very thirsty," the man said.

"And maybe he wasn't alone," Fargo thought aloud.

"I see nobody with him," the innkeeper said with another shrug.

"Couldn't he have brought somebody in the rear door without you seeing him? The stage was right against the door," Fargo asked.

Santo frowned in thought. "I suppose so. I am up front mostly," he conceded.

"And he could have brought someone down before you woke up this morning," Fargo said.

"I guess so, *señor*," Santo agreed.

Fargo took a handful of coins and put them on the table as he finished his coffee and strode back to the room to get his saddle. It was time for another look at that empty Concord, he muttered inwardly. It was time to see whether his sixth sense had been as acute as it usually was.